## Pastor Mike's talk on marriage must have put crazy thoughts in Andy's mind.

"Earth to Andy." Lori waved a hand in front of his face.

He leaned back in his chair, away from her teasing and the suddenly overpowering scent of her fruity perfume. Combined with the aroma hovering in the shop, she smelled like a chocolate-covered strawberry. What was wrong with him?

This was *Lori*, the girl who passed hastily scribbled notes to him during church with smiley faces, asking where they were going for lunch. The girl who ganged up with his youth group to spray him with silly string one summer morning on his way into the office. The girl who knew most of his secrets, brought him back to reality when he got prideful, and encouraged him when he felt like a failure.

The girl who'd been so close to his side for so many years that he'[...] directly in front of h[...]

**Books by Betsy St. Amant**

Love Inspired

*Return to Love*
*A Valentine's Wish*

## BETSY ST. AMANT

loves polka-dot shoes, chocolate and sharing the good news of God's grace through her novels. She has a bachelor's degree in Christian communications from Louisiana Baptist University and is actively pursuing a career in inspirational writing. Betsy resides in northern Louisiana with her husband and daughter and enjoys reading, kickboxing and spending quality time with her family.

# A Valentine's Wish
## Betsy St. Amant

Steeple
Hill®

Published by Steeple Hill Books™

STEEPLE HILL BOOKS

Steeple
Hill®

Recycling programs
for this product may
not exist in your area.

ISBN-13: 978-0-373-87581-8

A VALENTINE'S WISH

www.SteepleHill.com

**Printed in U.S.A.**

"O taste and see that the Lord is good."
—*Psalms* 34:8

To my husband, Brandon—you'll always be my Valentine. And most importantly, to Jesus Christ, the true lover of our souls—thank you for the gift.

## Acknowledgments

Every author needs a pack of personal superheroes, and my bunch is the best! Special thanks to super agent Tamela Hancock Murray, super editor Emily Rodmell, and super crit bud Georgiana Daniels. Also, thanks to Lori Chally for letting me borrow your first name, your love for shoes and your penchant for chocolate for the heroine in this story! Love you, sister!

# Chapter One

Unemployed. Single. And out of brownie mix.

Lori Perkins tapped her nails against the open pantry door. Canned vegetables and peanut butter crackers were nowhere near sufficient for this kind of low. She rested her forehead against the frame and blew a strand of dark hair out of her eyes. It really wasn't her fault—well, maybe two of the three problems were. She probably shouldn't have quit her job at the aquarium gift shop before the administrative position across town was a done deal, and she definitely should have gone to the grocery store before her chocolate stash ran out. But her single status was most certainly not of her own choosing. Add the fact that Valentine's Day was mere weeks away, and it became official. She was broke, hungry and destined to be alone.

The cordless phone on the counter jangled a shrill ring, and Lori snatched it up while peering one more time at the contents of her bottom shelf. "Hello?"

"Lori? I can barely hear you. Are you in a tunnel?" It was her friend Andy Stewart, the youth pastor at her church, L'Eglise de Grace.

She stretched one arm toward the back of the shelf. "No. The pantry."

"Searching for chocolate, I assume."

"Funny." So what if she'd become a little predictable over the years? Lori fumbled around a jar of peanut butter and felt a crinkly wrapper. Maybe a forgotten candy bar? No, just another package of crackers. She let out a huff. Was a little chocolate too much to ask for a girl having one of the worst days of her life?

"Are you all right? I can call back."

Lori shut the pantry door with a loud click and rested her back against the wooden panels. "I need chocolate."

"You're out? How is that possible?"

"Gracie helped me finish the last of my emergency stash."

"And she didn't refill?"

"There wasn't time before the wedding." She supposed Gracie had more important things on her mind at the time, like planning a honeymoon. Excited as she was for her friend's new life, Lori couldn't help the flicker of jealousy in her stomach. Happily-ever-after endings apparently weren't meant for everyone—her ex, Jason, had proven that point well enough.

She slammed the brakes on her runaway train of negative thoughts. "Look, is there a point to this conversation, or can I finish my desperate search for relief now?"

"Ouch. Bad day?"

"Did you not hear me say I'm out of chocolate?" *Men*. The cute ones cheated, and the funny ones were dense. Take Andy, for example. They'd been practically best friends for how long now—two years? Three? And he'd never once considered Lori as anything more.

Though it was probably for the best. If bitter thoughts of Jason still crept in her subconscious, she wasn't ready for more. The need for chocolate intensified, and Lori squeezed her eyes shut. Maybe if she pretended hard enough she could—

Andy cleared his throat. "How about I bring over some chocolate doughnuts? I have something I need to talk to you about."

Lori stopped the *no* from automatically rolling off her tongue. She preferred to indulge in her chocolate bad moods by herself, but without the chocolate, the bad-mood part sounded pretty lonely. "Fine. See you in twenty."

"You're late." Lori snatched the box of doughnuts from Andy's hands and left him to shut the front door of her town house. Hopefully, the smile she flashed softened her short words. She didn't want to sound ungrateful, but she had yet to consume any chocolate. She'd be nice after the sugar melted in her system.

Lori ripped two napkins free from the stand and tossed one in Andy's general direction as he leaned against the kitchen counter. "Thanks, by the way." She ripped open the box and inhaled the warm chocolate scent. Finally.

"I only brought a dozen. Hope that's enough." Andy's cheeky grin didn't even bother Lori as the sugar dissolved on her tongue. *Bliss.* She reached for a second.

"You know, some people might call this constant craving of yours an addiction." He plucked a pastry from the box and tore it in half before stuffing one piece in his mouth. Chocolate smeared down the side of his clean-shaven jaw.

"You tell me this like I'm supposed to care." She grinned back and licked her fingers, deciding not to tell him about the mess on his face. Call it revenge for that time she volunteered at the youth service and unknowingly wore a dot of whipped cream on the end of her nose for two hours.

Andy snorted and tossed a swoop of blond hair out of his eyes. "It's a miracle you don't weigh a ton. Even my youth group doesn't eat like this."

Lori patted her flat stomach. "Good genes. Now, did you come here to discuss my appetite, or was there something else?" She went for another doughnut, dodging Andy's attempt to swat her hand. Forget endorphins from exercise. This was much easier.

Andy swiped his face with his napkin before crumpling it

into a ball. "I have a question for you, and ironically, it involves chocolate."

"Mmm, go on." At this rate Lori could almost forget her bad day. Should she go for a fourth? Her stomach rolled a negative answer, and she quickly tucked the lid back into the corners of the box. Breakfast for tomorrow—hopefully Andy didn't think he was taking any of these babies home with him.

Andy leaned forward and rested his elbows on the counter. "You remember my aunt Bella?"

"Of course. She owns that chocolate shop in the French Quarter." Lori hopped onto the bar stool next to Andy. "I'm in there every time I have enough spare change for a chocolate crocodile. Those things are delicious." Though due to her current unemployed status, spare change might soon be a thing of the past. She sobered.

"Right. Well, she's had a family emergency. Her sister in Shreveport needs around-the-clock care for a while. She has to leave the store with someone temporarily, and I thought of you when she asked if anyone in the church needed a job."

Lori raised an eyebrow. "Why me?"

Andy ticked the reasons off on his fingers. "You ran the gift shop at the aquarium for years. You have an associate's degree in business. And you're currently unemployed, unless something has changed since you told me yesterday. Besides, she's got a college student working part-time, so you wouldn't be thrown in there alone."

Lori nibbled her bottom lip, tasting the leftover remains of doughnut. Working in a chocolate boutique. It did sound perfect for her—but would her fast metabolism hold up to that much temptation? She squinted. Maybe if she limited herself to one piece a day…

"Lori? Are you still with me, or have you slipped into a doughnut-induced coma?" Andy waved his hand in front of her face.

She slapped his hand away. "I'm debating."

"Another pro/con list?"

"No, I gave those up after my list suggested it'd be smart to go jogging after eating a double cheeseburger." For now, anyway. She'd never actually be able to give up her beloved lists.

Andy winced. "Sorry I asked. So?"

So. Working around that rich, tantalizing aroma all day, every day. Bringing joy to people's faces with bonbons and caramel creams and chocolate-dipped marshmallows…and better yet, distracting herself from the fact she hadn't had a date in over a year.

Lori smiled. "Count me in."

"A pie in the face is only funny on TV, Jeremy. Not during church." Andy tried to keep a straight face as he studied the cream-covered teenage duo in front of him. Tufts of meringue rose from the top of the football player's dark hair and peaked beside his ears. "In my opinion, you sort of had the payback coming."

"Ha!" Haley, Jeremy's off-again, on-again girlfriend, stuck out her tongue. Strawberry-pie filling smeared down the side of her cheek, and one hip remained cocked, a sure sign the little spitfire was mad. She tossed her pastry-streaked braids over her shoulder. "I told you he wouldn't get me in trouble."

"On the contrary." Andy struggled to keep his lips from turning up. He couldn't laugh in front of them. Two of his favorite youth-group members—but also the two responsible for those silver hairs he found in his sideburns last week. He cleared his throat. "You're both cleaning up the kitchen in the gym from this little war, and you're on door-greeting duty for three weeks."

Relief etched across Jeremy's tanned features as he relaxed against the door frame. "That seems fair."

"Did I mention you're also going to bring dessert to next Wednesday night's youth service?"

Jeremy's mouth opened.

"Since this pie was sacrificed on the altar of fun and games, it only seems fair." Andy crossed his arms over his chest, daring him to argue.

Haley laughed and pointed at Jeremy. "You have to—"

"I meant both of you."

Her arm fell to her side, and she glared.

"I want it homemade. Together." That would teach them to get along. "And while you're at it, why not make it red and white to celebrate the upcoming holiday?" He bit back another smile. Maybe frosting hearts on a few cupcakes would get the two of them back in their disgustingly lovey-dovey yet non-food-throwing stage in time for Valentine's Day. He definitely didn't want to deal with two heartbroken teenagers.

Jeremy's eyes widened with panic. A frown dimpled Haley's forehead. "Homemade? We can't—"

"Dishrags are in the drawer beside the fridge. Better get to cleaning." Andy sat in his chair, ducking his head and dismissing them as he pretended to shuffle through the youth calendar on his desk. He pursed his lips. If they didn't leave *now*—

Footsteps sounded down the hall, Haley's angry mutterings at Jeremy drifting in their wake. Andy palmed his hand over his mouth and finally released his laugh. What a couple. If those two made it down the aisle one day, he could only imagine the cake-feeding moment at the wedding reception.

Too bad Lori didn't get to see their argument. Scratch that—she'd probably have started the food fight. But she'd left early from the youth service, abandoning her usual after-church chaperoning duty to meet Aunt Bella for a job interview.

Andy leaned back in his chair, the leather creaking in protest, and crossed his arms behind his head. Lori should be an easy hire—she'd be great at the position, and Aunt Bella was in a hurry to head north to her family. It seemed like a good match. Hopefully he'd know soon.

A knock sounded on his open office door. Senior Pastor Mike Kinsey held up one hand in a wave. "Andy. I'm glad you're still here."

Andy quickly stood. "Come on in, Pastor." He motioned toward the empty chair across his desk. "Have a seat."

"Those two…" Mike gestured toward the direction Haley and Jeremy had gone and shook his head with a slight smile. "They must keep you busy."

"They still arguing out there?"

"Something about cakes versus brownies." Mike sat.

Andy settled into his chair. "It's a long, messy story."

"I can imagine." The smile slowly faded from Mike's face, and his expression sobered. "Listen, Andy. There's something I need to discuss with you."

"That serious?"

Mike shrugged, but the crease between his brows gave him away.

Andy drew a steadying breath. Maybe one of the youth had gotten into some minor trouble. Or maybe the pastor was discouraged about the youth group's sudden drop in attendance these past few weeks. One solemn conversation didn't necessarily mean his job was on the line. He flexed his fingers in his lap.

"I take it you heard about the youth minister who was fired last week?"

Andy nodded. The incident had been on the news for days. A youth pastor at a church across town had been arrested for inappropriate conduct with a minor—one of his own youth-group members. The ordeal had made Andy sick.

"It's created talk in our church."

Andy raised one eyebrow. "Talk?"

"There's no easy way to say this." Mike tugged at his tie. The fluorescent light above their heads buzzed, nearly deafening in the sudden silence. Andy's fingers found a pencil on his desktop, and he gripped it hard. *Say it, just say it.*

"Some of the parents of our youth have made comments about your single status." Mike released his tie, and his hands fell limply to his lap.

"Comments?"

"They feel it creates a bad image. That you'd be a better minister if you were, well…married."

*"Married?"* he couldn't stop parroting. His own church doubted his integrity? The room darkened around the edges, and he sucked in a tight breath. "That's… Sir, I—"

"It sounds harsher than they mean it. They just want to protect you."

Andy's throat constricted. "And their children."

Mike's shoulders drooped. "That, too."

"They don't trust me?" His stomach felt like he'd swallowed the mirrored paperweight on his desk.

"You've proven yourself to their kids over and over. They're just paranoid right now. That scandal really stirred everyone up."

Apparently. Andy pulled one arm across his chest in a stretch and tried to ignore the way the room closed in like a claustrophobic's worst nightmare. Marriage. Like it was that easy to find the perfect woman with whom he wanted to spend the rest of his life.

His eyes drifted to the framed photo on his desk, taken last summer during youth camp in Baton Rouge. Lori stood front and center next to his gang of miscreants, all wearing big smiles and matching yellow tees. His eyes lingered on Lori's image, then quickly darted back to Mike.

"With all due respect, sir, doesn't the congregation realize that if it were so easy, I'd be married by now? It's not like I particularly enjoy going home every night to hot dogs and reality TV reruns."

"I can imagine. However…" Mike shifted uncomfortably in his chair.

Andy's stomach rolled again. Something was up. He braced

his elbows against the edge of the desk. "What are you really saying, Pastor?"

Mike twisted his gold wedding band around on his finger. "That the church board would like for you to get serious about finding a wife." He cleared his throat, then met Andy's gaze. "The sooner the better."

## Chapter Two

"What have I gotten myself into?" The whispered words drifted toward the pink-painted ceiling, riding the wake of a delicious chocolate aroma. Lori planted her hands on the glass display counter and eyed the cozy boutique. Black iron tables for two snuggled in various corners of the shop, inviting patrons to linger over their coffee and chocolate. Fresh roses offered a splash of pink in the center of each table, and the black-and-white tiled floor appeared freshly scrubbed. Bella had left the Chocolate Gator in pristine condition—Lori hoped she'd be able to return it in the same shape after nearly two months.

Nice as the New Orleans native was, Lori couldn't help but wonder if Andy's aunt Bella was slightly off her rocker. In her mid-fifties, she practically oozed grace and charm with a Southern flair—just like her boutique. But trusting a near stranger with her business, on the sole recommendation of her only nephew, seemed a bit crazy. Sure, there was a chef and a college student working part-time at the register a few days a week, and yes, Lori had often chatted with Bella while buying those signature chocolate crocodiles, but was that enough to merit such responsibility?

Lori strode to the front door and flipped the white cardboard sign to read Open. She shouldn't complain. Less than a week ago she didn't have a job, and now she was running one of the trendiest boutiques in New Orleans—not to mention total access to those yummy little milk chocolate and caramel crocodiles. She sneaked a glance at the chocolates arranged on doilies in the display case. Even with her discount, she just might end up eating her paycheck. Literally.

The swinging kitchen door splayed open, nearly banging into the wall behind the register. Lori jumped as a tall, olive-skinned man in a white apron strode across the floor toward her. This had to be the chef Bella had mentioned. It would be in Lori's best interest to impress him, so that any reports going back to Bella would be positive. She offered a nervous smile. "Hi, I'm—"

"Lori, yes. The new manager Bella sent." He grinned and dipped into a low bow, the white strings of his apron dangling close to the ground. The scent of mint chocolate drifted to Lori's nose. "I am Edmondo Renardo Rossi, but you may call me Monny."

"It's nice to meet you, Monny." She offered her hand.

"The pleasure is all mine." He caught her palm and squeezed. "We shall make—what do they say?—beautiful chocolate together." He winked.

A half snort, half laugh escaped Lori's mouth, and she tried to cover it with a cough. When Bella told Lori about the chef, she must have forgotten to mention he was the Italian drama king. "Wow, your accent is strong."

Monny released her hand and straightened his shoulders with pride. "It should be. I am from Napoli, and am here in America to learn Cajun cuisine and desserts. My family owns a business and wanted me to bring new cultures to our restaurant."

"I see. So you're learning the ropes on desserts right now, apparently." Lori motioned toward the streaks of dried fudge on his apron.

"Ropes?" Two brown eyebrows meshed together as one.

Lori pointed toward the kitchen. "Learning how to bake."

She pantomimed stirring in a bowl, then felt ridiculous. He didn't need sign language; he obviously spoke English. Her cheeks warmed.

"Ah, *si.*" Monny kissed his fingertips in a broad gesture. "Before Bella hired me, I worked at the Gumbo Shop. You Southern Americans, you like the spices."

The bell on the door tinkled. Lori jerked. She'd gotten so distracted trying to decipher Monny's accent, she'd forgotten she was there to work. She hadn't even opened the register yet. Or fanned the pink paper napkins on the counter as Bella said she did every morning. Or more importantly, sampled a crocodile before they sold out.

"I'll have my usual." An elderly, slightly hunched gentleman in a pinstripe suit hobbled toward the counter, a heavy cane accentuating his steps. A cool winter breeze floated in behind him, stirring Lori's hair. The door shut with a clank.

"Ah, customers. Time to work." Monny lightly patted Lori's cheek before disappearing into the kitchen. *"Ciao."*

"Wait, what's his usual?" But Monny was gone in a puff of flour and charm. Lori hurried into position behind the register, shaking her head to wrench back to reality.

"Good morning." She put on her best smile. "I'm taking over for Bella—"

"Who are you?" the old man barked, lips nearly hidden behind a thick gray mustache. "Where's Bella?"

"She had a family emergency. I'm Lor—"

"I said what's your name, dearie? You deaf?"

Lori winced. "No, sir, I said my name is—"

"Ah, forget it. Young people have no manners nowadays." He thumped one gnarled hand on the counter. "Give me my usual."

"I'm afraid I don't know—"

"Don't tell me you're out of black coffee and dark chocolate raspberries."

Lori exhaled for the first time in what felt like minutes. "Of course not. Right away, sir." She reached for the coffeepot—the empty coffeepot. "Uh, just a minute." She opened the white cabinet doors under the coffee station. Where were all the beans? And how was she supposed to work that glittering monstrosity of a coffee machine?

Panic cramped her stomach in time to the impatient tapping of Grouchy Man's cane. She was going to fail on her first day of work. Make that her first ten minutes of work. She'd never get to eat chocolate again. Why couldn't the other girl, the college student, what's-her-name-with-the-eyebrow-ring, have been working today?

Lori shoved her hair out of her eyes with an impatient flick, then paused. The list. Bella had said she would leave a list of instructions in the register since she hadn't had an opportunity to train Lori in person. Anything else she needed she could ask the chef or Eyebrow-Ring Girl or could call Bella's cell.

Lori unlocked the register and grabbed the list with a triumphant hand. Redemption, in the form of neat penmanship and sheets of lined notebook paper. *Thank You, Lord.* She skim-read until she found the section labeled Coffee.

The instructions were two inches long.

Lori licked her lips, darted a glance at the cappuccino machine staring menacingly down at her and then at Grouchy Man. "Why don't you take a seat, and I'll serve you when it's ready?"

She couldn't tell if the frown was new, or if his wrinkles were permanently knit that way, but regardless, Grouchy Man stomped his cane toward a nearby table and planted himself in a chair, arms crossed.

Lori turned back toward the machine and drew a fortifying breath. She was so having a chocolate crocodile after this.

Andy tried the handle on the door of the Chocolate Gator. Locked. The hours posted informed him the shop closed at six, and it was fifteen past. He cupped his hands around his eyes and peered through the glass into the dim boutique. He could barely make out Lori's sprawled form at a table, one arm hanging limply over the back of her seat. Her legs were crossed, and she rubbed one bare foot with her free hand. Red high-heel shoes lay on the floor by her chair.

He winced. High heels on the first day at a new job? Big mistake—but knowing Lori and her accessory fetish, she'd be back in a different pair of equally ridiculous shoes tomorrow, and probably sporting a matching purse. He knocked on the glass.

Lori waved and gestured at her feet. As in, she wasn't about to get up. Part of him couldn't blame her; the other part wanted to point to her shoes and yell *duh*. He knocked louder.

"Coming!" an Italian accent bellowed through the glass. Andy jumped. The door was flung open to reveal a tall, dark-haired guy about his own age, maybe late twenties. *"Ciao."*

"Uh, *ciao.*" Andy stepped over the threshold, taking in the chocolate smeared on the sleeves of the man's white shirt and the flour dusting the top of his shoes. "I'm Bella's nephew, Andy Stewart."

"Ah, *si!* You are the one who secured this angel a job." He gestured toward Lori, who grinned and offered an innocent shrug. Angel? Apparently this guy had never experienced Lori's temper—or witnessed her reaction to an empty doughnut box.

Andy cleared his throat. "I guess I am. And you are?" The chef, obviously. But Andy wanted a name—and he really wanted the odd twisting sensation in his stomach that began the moment this dude called Lori an angel to quit.

"Edmondo, or Monny. I cook with Bella."

They shook hands, Andy's grip a bit tighter than necessary. He forced his palm to relax. "Nice to meet you." His aunt told him months ago about her new chef from overseas, but failed to mention he was this young—and this Italian. Hopefully Lori wasn't one of those crazy girls who got all excited hearing a foreign accent….

"Monny, say that thing you said earlier." Lori flipped her long hair over her shoulder, the light returning to her tired eyes. "About chocolate."

"You mean *cioccolata, mi cara*." He winked.

Andy's eyes narrowed. *Cara?* From the look in Edmondo's eyes, that term of endearment definitely didn't mean coworker. He pulled out the chair across from Lori and sank into it, the screech against the tile floor interrupting the annoying flow of foreign words from Edmondo. Just his luck, the guy could probably make the phone book sound romantic.

"So, how was your first day?" He scooted a vase of flowers to the side so he could see Lori's face. She was *his* friend before this guy's, and he needed to tell her what happened at the church. Monny could wait.

*"Thanks for the job, Bella. You can't train me in the shop? No problem, I'm a quick learner. I can figure it out, Bella. Of course I can make coffee, Bella,"* Lori mocked, her hands covering her face.

"That good, huh?"

"Yes." She peeked through her fingers at Andy and smiled. "But I loved every minute of it."

He laughed and tugged her hands down to the table. "You've got flour in your hair."

"Thanks for that, Monny." She pulled free and patted at her head.

Monny flipped the lock on the front door and grinned. "Just be glad it wasn't the raspberry crème." He paused at their table. "I'll leave through the back so you won't have to lock the front door again. See you tomorrow."

"Bye." Lori wiggled her fingers in a wave. "Maybe tomorrow will be easier since I'll have help at the front."

"You did a wonderful job."

"Only because of your help." She smiled.

Andy's stomach rolled. Was Lori flirting back with this guy?

The fake charm practically oozed from Monny's tanned skin. Lori couldn't be actually falling for it…right? He wadded a stray napkin into a ball and clenched it in his fist as Monny disappeared through the kitchen doors.

Lori met Andy's gaze with a slight frown, gesturing at his white-knuckled grip. "Are you okay?"

He dropped the napkin and opened his mouth, and then hesitated before answering. If *okay* included his job being all but threatened, and this sudden burst of jealousy over one of his best friends, then sure. He shook his head to clear the random thoughts. Pastor Mike's talk on marriage must have put crazy thoughts in his mind.

"Earth to Andy." Lori waved a hand in front of his face. "I thought I was the one who was worn out. Don't make me put you in the ring with that cappuccino machine." She wiggled her eyebrows up and down. "You might not come out alive."

He leaned back in his chair, away from her teasing and the suddenly overpowering scent of her fruity perfume. Combined with the aroma hovering in the shop, she smelled like a chocolate-covered strawberry. What was wrong with him? This was Lori, the girl who passed hastily scribbled notes to him during church with smiley faces asking where they were going for lunch. The girl who ganged up with his youth group to spray him with Silly String one summer morning on his way into the office. The girl who knew most of his secrets, brought him back to reality when he got prideful and encouraged him when he felt like a failure.

The girl who'd been so close to his side for so many years that he'd failed to see what was directly in front of him.

Andy stared at Lori as if for the first time. Long brown hair swept into a partial ponytail. Eyes twinkling with laughter despite the fatigue lining the edges. A few freckles spattered across her nose that she never tried to cover with makeup. Lori.

His best friend…and the woman who just might make the senior church staff—and him—very, very happy.

His lips spread in a slow smile. "Actually, yes. I think I am all right now."

# Chapter Three

Lori drew a deep breath of chocolate-scented air and closed her eyes. Tuesday. A new day, a fresh start, a second chance to succeed.

Or fail miserably.

Her eyes popped open. She had to think positively—surely her second day would be better than the first. The part-time worker, Summer Pierce, would be there after noon to help run the register and bag orders. Besides, Lori now knew what Mr. Grouchy's "usual" was, and she'd won more rounds than she'd lost with the coffeemaker. It couldn't get any harder than that, right?

The sound of Monny's melodic humming from the kitchen lightened her mood, and Lori swayed in rhythm as she fanned Bella's signature pink and black napkins on the counter. She'd taken interior-design classes in college, and she really appreciated Bella's decorating skills. Everything in the shop blended, but didn't match. That was important in drawing the eye and creating an environment.

Lori's eyes narrowed as she took in the room. Had Bella ever considered selling other coordinating products in her store? The setup was perfect for merchandise. Pink and black mugs, for example, or mini stuffed animals carrying bags of chocolate.

Even logo purses would probably sell, if done in the shop's signature colors.

She reached for a pad of paper under the register and a pencil. Maybe she could jot down a few ideas to mention once Bella came back. Or better yet, create a pro/con list to show Bella how well her ideas would work.

"Lori, *mi cara!*"

Lori jerked at her name, still not used to it being followed by Monny's ever-present "my dear" tag. "Coming!" She dropped the pad and pencil and pushed through the swinging kitchen door. Much as she hated to admit it, Monny's attention the last two days had soothed the raw spot left from Jason's betrayal, and the ache from Andy's lack of interest. If a cute Italian chef was possibly attracted to her, who cared what her ex or her best friend thought, right?

She hurried into the kitchen. Monny stood over a giant pot of churning ingredients. "I'm making fudge. Will you stir this while I check on the sponge cake? *Prego?*"

"Sure." She took the long wooden spoon and ran it through the white mixture. "What's in here?"

Monny donned an oven mitt. "Sugar, milk, vanilla…and a secret ingredient or two." He yanked open the oven door with a smile. "Bella would not be happy if I told."

Lori stirred the thickening concoction faster, trying to ignore the twinge of hurt in her stomach. She couldn't exactly blame Bella for not trusting her with the shop's secrets. It was enough she trusted Lori with the store itself. Besides, it wasn't Bella who refused to tell her, just Monny doing what he thought was the proper thing. Right?

Her thoughts trailed off. The oven door shut, and Monny called instructions over the sound of the kitchen's whirring exhaust fan. "And add the chocolate, in the bowl to your left."

Lori jerked back to attention. She grabbed the mixing bowl, full of chopped chocolate pieces, and added it to the boiling mixture in the pot. She stirred harder, hoping Monny hadn't noticed her zoning out. Not that she was trying to impress him—was she? She chewed her bottom lip, the spoon slowing in her hand. She hadn't been on a date in so long she'd forgotten the rules of flirting. It was all Andy's fault. If he'd just paid attention to her in the way she wanted him to, instead of being such an oblivious *guy,* maybe they could have—

"Watch out!"

Monny's warning cry came too late. Thick chocolate bubbles popped. Lori shrieked. Chocolate sprayed, barely missing her face. She stepped back, wielding the wooden spoon. The thick mixture dripped off the edge of the spoon and onto her clothing. She shrieked again as the warmth seeped through her thin sweater.

"Hot!" Lori fanned her shirt away from her body. The spoon clattered to the floor. Monny ran toward the pot as more bubbles popped. He ducked as one splattered the oven backsplash, and reached for the burner. Another bubble burst and sprayed his wrist. He mumbled in Italian and turned off the burner. His other hand with the oven mitt moved the steaming pot away from the heat.

Monny turned to Lori, chocolate coating his apron. He slowly took off the mitt, his chest expanding as he drew a deep breath. "*Mi cara,* I said to remove from heat before adding the chocolate."

"Oops." Lori felt a flush creep up her neck. Or maybe it was just the result of her hot-chocolate dance. "I must not have heard that part. I'm sorry."

"No problem. It will be—what do you say?—Saveable."

"Salvageable?"

"*Si.*" Monny picked up the spoon from the floor and tossed it into the deep stainless-steel sink. The corners of his lips crinkled into a smile. "One disaster averted. Let's see if we can make this fudge—"

"The cake!" Lori gestured wildly to the oven behind Monny, where smoke started to seep from the edges.

Monny grabbed the oven mitt again and wrenched open the door. Smoke billowed. He hefted the pan from inside, and it landed on the counter with a clatter. The chocolate batter had bubbled over onto the oven rack and burned. He stared listlessly at the hardened, crusty shell of what was supposed to be one of the Chocolate Gator's best-selling products.

Lori waved one hand at the dissipating smoke and coughed. "Maybe we can still sell it and call it Cajun?"

Andy stared at the pen in his hand, willing it to obey. "Write. Something, anything—just write!" But no words formed on the card lying on his desk. Big surprise. Penning thoughts to your good friend turned best friend turned love interest wasn't exactly easy.

He dropped the pen with a groan and flopped back in his office chair. Maybe this wasn't such a great idea. Last night, sitting in his recliner and flipping channels on the TV, the concept of sending secret gifts seemed ingenious. Surely it'd break the ice between him and Lori and warm her up to the idea of being more than friends. Hey, it worked for the guy in the Lifetime movie, didn't it? But now it just seemed ridiculous. Lori said herself a year ago that she was through with the dating game after her ex-fiancé hurt her so badly.

The church staff was being unfair. Like finding true love was so easy. Like discovering the one person you wanted to spend the rest of your life with was this no-big-deal, everyday occurrence. Maybe he should forget the idea of finding a woman and remove himself from the game as Lori had done. Being a bachelor wasn't *that* bad—although he could stand a home-cooked meal or two. And someone to remind him not to leave wet towels on the bedroom carpet so his room wouldn't smell so moldy the next day. And it wouldn't be awful to have someone to fight with over leaving the toothpaste cap off or whose turn it was to wash dishes or how much spice to put in the jambalaya.

But was it worth this kind of headache?

He grabbed a Hershey's Kiss from the bowl on his counter—the bowl he kept for Lori when she was hanging out at the church—and let his eyes drift back to the greeting card in front of him. It was catchy and corny, just Lori's thing. Two grinning cartoon characters with big moony eyes, one shooting pulsing heart beams toward the other with a bow and arrow. The text read Cupid Ain't Got Nothing on Me. But what could he write underneath? And wouldn't she recognize his handwriting?

The guy in the movie hadn't had these kinds of problems.

Andy raked one hand through his hair. At least the bouquet of daisies and stargazer lilies would be a winner. Lori told him a year ago that lilies were her favorite flower because she figured they were God's favorite, too. When he questioned her reasoning, she simply said a flower that smelled that strongly was obviously trying to waft its aroma toward Heaven.

He sniffed and fought a sneeze. She wasn't kidding. He grabbed for a tissue seconds before the allergy attack began. Leave it to Lori to prefer the least subtle flower in all of nature. The sooner he figured out this card thing and delivered the gift, the sooner he could breathe again. Although Lori's potential rejection would probably suck the life from their friendship. He wondered if he should even risk this.

The phone jangled on his desk, and he eagerly snatched it up. Any distraction was better than hovering over this greeting card, feeling like a poetic failure. "Youth pastor's office, this is Andy."

"Andy, my favorite nephew." His aunt's voice rang through the line with her usual flair of Southern charm.

He laughed at their long-standing argument. "Aunt Bella, I'm your only nephew."

"*Psh*. Details." He could just imagine her flipping her manicured hand in the air as if brushing off such a concept. "Listen, dear, I'm at the airport and don't have much time. I need a favor."

"Sure, Aunt Bella. It's the least I can do after you hooked Lori up with a job." Andy rolled a pencil between his fingers.

"That's why I'm calling. I have no doubt Lori can handle the store. Our quick interview together and her résumé proved her competent." Bella drew in a deep breath. "But I don't know her very well, and since you obviously do, I was hoping you might keep an eye on things while I'm gone. Be there to lend a hand if she needs it. Unofficially, of course."

"Of course. You'd hate to cut another paycheck." Andy grinned. "Boy, you know good and well—"

"I'm just kidding, Aunt Bella." Andy dropped the pencil on his desk and leaned back in his chair. "I'm happy to help, for free. I'm sure Lori won't mind if I hang around the shop a bit."

Bella paused. "I was also sort of hoping you wouldn't tell her."

Andy swallowed. Not tell Lori? That was sure to blow up in his face later. "Aunt Bella, I—"

"I don't want Lori to get paranoid about my faith in her abilities. I just want someone to keep a watch out and be nearby if there is an emergency." Bella's voice turned pleading. "I'm talking about a few pop-in visits, a few phone calls. Nothing you probably wouldn't do for her anyway."

She was right about that—of course Andy would visit Lori at work. But if Lori found out about the ulterior motive... Andy winced. It wouldn't be pretty.

Her voice was beginning to sound far away. "I've got to go, dear. The signal is fading. Just say yes."

Andy released his breath, regretting the words he knew he had to speak. "No problem, Aunt Bella. I'll keep an eye on Lori and the store for you. Don't worry about a thing." He squeezed his eyes closed as he disconnected the call. Maybe Lori wouldn't ever have to find out. Maybe he could stay subtle enough that she wouldn't feel that he was doing anything more than being a good friend.

His eyes drifted back to the still-unsigned greeting card. A good friend with a secret motive that had nothing to do with the store or his aunt.

"Pastor Andy?"

Andy looked up from the card. Haley stood in his open office door. "Haley! What are you doing out of school?" He swiped the card into his desk drawer and slammed it shut.

She slowly approached his desk, brow furrowed. "What do you mean? It's after three o'clock."

"Are you serious?" Andy glanced at his watch—3:22 p.m. The afternoon sun streaming through the slanted blinds confirmed that the world continued to revolve…and not around him. Had he really been sitting there staring at Lori's gift for almost two hours? He groaned again.

Haley plopped down in the chair across from his and smoothed her cheerleading uniform over her legs. "I came by to tell you Jeremy and I tried making a strawberry cake for the youth service tomorrow. But he can't cook at all. He totally ruined our practice cake."

"You made a practice cake?" He bit back a grin. Somehow, he didn't picture Jeremy hanging out in a kitchen more than absolutely necessary. But at least they were working together and learning teamwork, as was the goal.

"Tried to." Haley tossed one braid over her shoulder. "The whole thing tasted like glue." She wrinkled her nose.

He decided not to ask how she knew what glue tasted like. "And it's entirely Jeremy's fault because…?"

Haley stared, *duh* written all over her expression. "He was the one who stirred."

"I see." Andy rubbed his fingers over his eyes. *Note to self: pick up dessert for Wednesday night.* Maybe that was a good thing. He could swing by the Chocolate Gator, pick up some brownies and visit Lori. If he could find a way to secretly deliver the gift before the service tomorrow, then he could gauge her reaction while he was there.

He sat up straight in his chair. Finally, a plan. Now he just needed to figure out what to write on the card and how to deliver it to the shop. He frowned. There was the problem. He couldn't just stroll inside with a mustache and hat and plunk the vase on the counter. She'd see right through it.

Right through him. He shuddered. No, he wasn't ready for that yet. He needed to see how Lori responded before he could open himself to that kind of vulnerability. But who would take the gift and keep his secret? Who did he even trust with his secret? He drummed his nails on the desktop.

"Who are those for?" Haley leaned forward and brushed the petals of the lilies with her fingertips.

"Nobody." The abrupt dismissal rolled off his tongue before Andy could process how suspicious it sounded, and he winced. Maybe Haley wouldn't notice.

"Yeah, right." She stood and leaned over the vase for a better view. "You have a girlfriend or something?"

Or something. Andy coughed. "No, they're for…" He stopped. He couldn't lie to his own youth-group member. "A friend."

Haley winked. "A special friend?"

"Just a friend." Andy stood as well and gestured toward the open door. "Thanks for stopping by. Don't worry about getting the dessert. I'll let you guys slide this time." He'd probably pay for it later, but the last thing he needed was Haley snooping around and figuring out his plan. Despite her off-again, on-again status with Jeremy, the girl was a super romantic and had at one point tried to set everyone in the youth group up with someone else.

Haley stayed by the flowers, seemingly oblivious to his attempt at her dismissal. "Come on, who is it?" Her hand stilled on the petals. "Not Tawny."

"No, not Tawny."

Her breath exhaled in a whoosh, and she continued to fluff the arrangement. "Good. She's not your type."

Andy agreed. It was debatable if Tawny Sinclair was anyone's type, especially after what she did to his best friend,

Carter. Gracie and Carter's relationship was almost over before it began, thanks to Tawny's seductive meddling, but it had all worked out. At the end of the day, she was still a woman in need of God's grace, a more conservative wardrobe and a healthy relationship—just definitely not with him. Thankfully Tawny's youth-group volunteer days were long over.

"Then who are they for?"

Haley wouldn't quit. Andy came around the front of the desk and steered her toward the door. "Isn't it enough I'm letting you off dessert duty?"

"No." She grinned. "I'm a teenager, Pastor Andy. You know it's never enough. Come on, spill it."

"Never." He opened the door wider, and it caught the rug at their feet. He kicked to free it while Haley continued to meddle.

"I'll do Wednesday desserts for two weeks."

Andy straightened, feigning interest. "Make it four."

"Okay, four."

"Nope, still not telling." He grinned back.

"Pastor Andy!" She huffed.

"I'm not telling you, because there's nothing to tell." A headache started at his temples. Why did he suddenly feel like he was in high school himself? The girl was persistent—no wonder Jeremy looked frustrated all the time. Going against his girlfriend had to be tougher than any opposing school's quarterback.

"Will this tell me?" Haley dangled a small white card in front of his face.

The delivery card with Lori's name on it.

The blood rushed to Andy's head, and his temples pounded harder. When had she— He sucked in his breath. The little minx, when she'd been playing with the arrangement! He'd dodged a zillion buckets-over-the-door and glue-on-the-toilet-seat pranks, but this one he never saw coming.

"Haley, give me that card." He held out his hand, but she pranced out of his reach and lifted the flap.

"For Lori?" She squealed, then clamped one hand over her mouth. "That's so perfect. Why didn't I think of it? And just in time for Valentine's Day!"

His anger at her disobedience fled. "Perfect? You think so?" He quickly shook his head. Now he was encouraged at the approval of a high-schooler? Still, no one knew him and Lori better than the youth group.

"You guys would be great together." Haley handed over the delivery card. "And I won't tell. I promise. I want to help."

"How in the world could you possibly…" Andy stopped as an idea formed. He looped one arm around Haley's shoulders and leaned down. "Ever had experience as a delivery girl?"

# Chapter Four

Lori stared at the flowers sitting on the counter. Where'd they come from? She'd gone into the kitchen to ask Monny about sugar-free chocolates, and when she came back, the flowers had appeared in all their fuchsia and burgundy glory. The store was deserted, as it was almost closing time, so it couldn't have been a customer. Maybe Bella had ordered them for the display before she left for Shreveport.

"Summer? You know anything about these?" Doubtful. The twenty-year-old, multipierced college student usually had her nose buried in a magazine during the store's late-afternoon lull. Or was jamming with her iPod.

Summer straightened from her slump against the counter and shrugged a thin shoulder. The fluorescent lights above glinted off her eyebrow ring. "Beats me. I must have been in the stockroom. Though I'm surprised I didn't smell those things coming a mile away."

Lori inhaled the spicy aroma of the lilies as she searched for a card among the pristine leaves. Smell? That was too harsh a word for this fragrance. The flowers were so pretty they almost seemed fake. She plucked the card from the greenery and blinked twice. Her name, scrawled in unfamiliar handwriting.

"What is that strong smell…?" Monny stepped through the kitchen and stopped short as Lori held up the bouquet.

"Someone sent me flowers."

"I see that." He coughed and backed away. "Very nice."

"Stargazers, my favorites. But I don't know why someone would have sent them. It's not my birthday."

"Anniversary?"

Lori frowned. "Anniversary of what?"

"Don't tell me Americans don't celebrate *amore.*" Monny patted his apron over his heart and grinned, his teeth appearing extra white in contrast to his olive skin.

Summer snorted and turned back to her magazine, shaking her head.

"Of course we celebrate love." Lori paused. "But I'm not dating anyone."

Monny's smile seemed to brighten, and Lori quickly averted her eyes back to the flowers. Was the surprise gift from him? They barely knew each other. But why else would he be interested in her dating status?

A dried petal fell to the counter, and for the first time, Lori noticed another card lying under the vase, a full-sized envelope like one would buy at Hallmark. She tugged it free and slit the light blue flap with her fingernail, noting from the corner of her eye that Monny slipped back inside the kitchen. To hide his knowing smile when she read his card, or just to check the brownies?

She was silly to think he'd be interested in her. No, she only attracted men with fast words and lying lips, men who broke promises and cheated on their fiancées.

Lori pulled her lower lip between her teeth and read the card, the bitterness of the past tainting the cute message. No signature, other than the words YOUR SECRET ADMIRER written in big block letters, an obvious attempt to hide the owner's handwriting.

Would Monny send a corny note like this one? Everything

else he had said or done during their days working together had been smooth. Sauve. Sophisticated, like his accent. But who was to say he didn't have a silly side lurking beneath that savvy exterior? She really didn't know him at all.

Couldn't truly know any man at all.

She slid the card back into the envelope, then thought twice. She pulled it back out and, after making sure Summer wasn't watching, stood it open beside the cash register. Might be silly, but if Andy—the man she *wanted* to notice her—never would, at least she could appreciate romantic efforts from a coworker. Even if she had no intention of following through with them.

Lori set the vase in a prime spot on the counter, then grabbed a dust cloth and began to wipe down the display case. Monny started humming a tune from the kitchen, and the melodic sound blossomed a sprig of hope beneath her doubt. If Monny could be interested in her, who was to say Andy might not come around one day? She absently joined in the song under her breath, swaying slowly as she cleaned.

Andy stood outside the Chocolate Gator and hesitantly peered through the window. Lori stood at the counter, head ducked as she counted bills at the register. Strands of her long brown hair, pulled halfway back, skimmed her cheeks as she rhythmically placed bills into stacks. Her lips moved slightly as she counted to herself.

Andy drew a deep breath. He'd been unable to sleep well last night, wondering if he'd done the right thing by sending Haley as a delivery girl. What if she told his secret? What if she wasn't subtle enough? What if Lori saw her and put two and two together? He wasn't ready for Lori to know his thoughts, his plan—and he definitely wasn't ready for her to hear what Pastor Mike had suggested about his love life.

Maybe it was too late. Maybe Haley hadn't been able to take the flowers yesterday afternoon at all. Or maybe they'd already died. Maybe he'd killed them with his secrets and his schemes and…

No, if the stargazer lilies were already dead, it was no doubt they'd collapsed from their own aroma.

Andy shoved his hands in his pockets, then realized he needed them to open the door—unless he stayed outside, which seemed like a good option at this point. Lori knew nothing, and he hadn't invested anything in this wacky plan except for the forty-three dollars and twenty-seven cents he'd spent on the flowers. Forty-seven dollars, if he counted the card. He could check on Lori for his aunt another time and just go home, forget about it all.

And then what—forget about ever finding a wife? Forget about his job? Forget about the way Lori's smile wreaked havoc in his stomach and her playful punches stung his arm like a thousand arrows from Cupid's bow?

Not likely.

Andy stole a peek through the window again, and his heartbeat spiked. The vase of flowers was on the counter opposite where Lori stood, part of a display with wrapped chocolate bars. That had to mean she liked them, right?

Lori stuffed the money inside a deposit bag and shut the register drawer. His stomach clenched. If he didn't go inside now, she'd leave out the back and he'd never know what she really thought of the flowers. Not to mention the youth group wouldn't have any dessert after their service tonight.

He ran his palm over his hair, winced at its clamminess and knocked on the door before he could change his mind. Lori looked up from the display with surprise, then hurried over to unlock the door.

"Hey, there." Her smile warmed his insides like the winter sunshine had moments ago warmed his clothes. "I just closed up. You almost missed me."

He returned her smile, trying not to read too much into her

greeting. She had no idea—he'd almost missed her by a lot more than ten minutes. If it hadn't been for Pastor Mike and the church board, he might have missed her by a lifetime. How could he have never noticed the parade of nerves inside his stomach while in her presence all these years?

Andy suddenly realized he had yet to speak and cleared his throat. "Oh, right. I came to get a dessert for the youth service tonight. Sorry I'm late." He wouldn't have been if he hadn't stopped to second-guess himself the entire way here. But she didn't need that information.

Lori frowned. "You should have just called me. I could have brought it and saved you the trip."

Andy leaned casually against the counter. "Well, I was just going to, you know, say hi. Or whatever." He couldn't tell her about Bella's request. Hopefully Lori wouldn't require further explanation. He cleared his throat again to stall, his eyes scanning the area behind the display even though he wasn't exactly sure what he expected to see. The flowers were already out front and center. What better reaction could he hope for?

"You'll see me in a few hours." Lori pulled a plastic glove over her hand and slid open the display case. "Just because I'm a shop manager now doesn't mean I'm going to skip out on my responsibility to the youth group."

"Of course not." Andy rubbed at his throat. What was that lump doing there? Other than blocking everything he was trying so hard to say. "I never thought that."

"Good." Lori snapped the edge of her glove against her hand with a flourish. "What'll it be, sir?" She grinned.

He opened his mouth to order three dozen chocolate-filled crème cookies. But the words lingered on his lips, unspoken. The silly cartoon card was propped against the register, where Lori could easily see it all day.

His neck warmed, and he tugged at his polo collar. "Uh…"

Lori quirked an eyebrow, her hand hovering over the display, waiting to know which item to grab. "Sorry, we're fresh out of *uh*. I must have burned them with the sponge cake yesterday."

Andy shook his head to clear it, forcing his eyes not to dart back to the telltale card. Or was he reading more into it than he should? He suddenly remembered all the reasons why he hadn't dated in so long. This was complicated stuff. "What's a sponge cake?"

"It's supposed to be a very light, airy cake. But because of me, it was a very dark, hard cake."

"Bad day?"

"An eventful afternoon, to say the least." Lori snorted. "I think I still have fudge in my hair."

Andy's stomach clenched again. Fudge in her hair—did that mean a food fight? He imagined Lori and that smooth-talking Italian flinging batter and dough and laughing together in the kitchen, the camaraderie and teasing maybe leading to a kiss. He swallowed. "I thought that guy did all the cooking?"

"Monny does do all the baking. But I was helping out, and well—it was disastrous." Lori rolled her eyes. "I don't know how much inventory I wasted. I probably won't be doing much baking anymore."

Good. Andy cleared his throat. "Sorry you had a tough time."

"Oh, it's gotten better. Monny and Summer are showing me how things work. It's been fun."

Great. Private tutoring. He straightened his shoulders and tried to ignore the way his heart began a slow descent toward his toes. "I guess I'll take a few dozen of those cookies there." He tapped the display window with his finger and tried to cheer up. At least Lori seemed to like his gift. Otherwise she would have thrown the card in the trash, right?

"Here you go." Lori bagged his order, then tossed the used glove in a wastebasket and punched buttons on the register. "At least I haven't messed this part up yet. If Summer and I can keep this drawer balanced every night, then I won't feel I've failed Bella's business."

Andy handed her his business credit card and watched as she swiped it through the machine. "You'll be fine. You can do anything you put your mind to." Too bad she hadn't put her mind to dating him. Or had she? Did she suspect the gift was from him at all? He really should have talked to Haley and gotten the details of the drop-off before coming in here. If Lori had seen Haley with the flowers, the odds of Lori's figuring out who her secret admirer was were much higher.

He was getting another headache. Maybe this secret-admirer plan wasn't his best idea. Andy shoved the credit card back into his wallet and took the pink paper bag from Lori's outstretched hand. "Listen, Lori—"

"Guess what—"

They spoke at the same time. Andy gestured with his hand. "Ladies first." It would give him time to stall the truth.

Lori shoved loose strands of her hair behind her ears. "I was just going to say guess what happened today?"

"What? Another brownie blowout?" He grinned at her excitement. How had he never noticed how beautiful she was before?

She slugged him in the arm over the counter, and his easy smile faltered at her touch. "No, silly. I learned that lesson."

He tried to ignore the way his shoulder warmed under his sleeve. "I give up, then."

"I have a secret admirer."

Andy nearly choked on his own spit. *Play it cool, play it cool.* He rotated his shoulders and cracked his neck, mentally preparing his confession. Maybe her no-dating stage was nearing an end. Maybe she would consider him after all. "Really?"

Lori glanced over her shoulder. "Yep." Then she leaned over the counter to whisper, "And I think it might be Monny."

# Chapter Five

✎

Andy fiddled with the microphone attachment on the waistband of his jeans, turning the volume in his headpiece up, then down. Up, down. At least it made him look busy and hopefully hid the fact that he remained unable to keep his eyes off Lori. She hurried around the kitchen area in the back of the gymnasium, setting out plastic cups and piles of napkins for the after-service snack.

He should be thinking about the announcements he needed to make during the service, or about the sermon he was about to deliver to his dwindling youth group, but all he could focus on was the fact that Lori seemed thrilled about her secret admirer—which would be a good thing if she realized it was *him,* and not that Italian cheese-ball.

He cranked the volume up again, then quickly back down as the feedback threatened his ears. Maybe the church board was right—he would be less distracted if he had a wife, though not in the way they assumed. Ironically, he hadn't been distracted at all until they'd approached him about the matter and brought to light his interest in Lori. If Pastor Mike hadn't said those things in his office last week, Andy would probably be reviewing his sermon notes right now instead of wearing a callus in his thumb from all the volume switching....

"Pastor Andy, watch out!" A Nerf football whizzed past Andy's head with inches to spare. He jerked and turned to see Jeremy jogging after the renegade ball, head ducked low in embarrassment. "Sorry, I told Peter to go long," he called over his shoulder as he chased the blur of rolling blue sponge.

Andy glanced at the kitchen again in time to see Lori leaning over the counter, laughing so hard her hair nearly covered her face. "Let me guess. You never made the team?" she shouted through cupped hands.

Like he'd even had a chance at catching that pass. He just waved and offered a smile, probably a pretty goofy one since he could feel his neck flushing a little. She probably thought Monny could have caught that ball and mixed up cake batter all at the same time. *Women.*

Haley appeared at his side with a soda can. "Here, Pastor Andy. Lori told me to give you this. She said you looked like you could use it."

He could, but that wasn't the point. Was Lori being sweet or cracking on his lack of football skills? He couldn't tell, now that she was back to work in the kitchen. Either way, the cold drink would hopefully revive him enough to get through the service in one piece.

Andy took the can from Haley and popped the top. "Thanks. Did you see your boyfriend almost nail me in the head with a football, too?"

"No. But he's not my boyfriend anymore." She wrinkled her nose. "We broke up."

He took a long drag on the Coke. "Until tomorrow."

"No, this time it's for real."

"Okay, a week, then." Andy winked.

Haley crossed her arms over her chest. "I'm not kidding. He really made me mad. Love stinks."

He debated arguing the love point with her, but quickly realized he didn't have nearly enough time before the service started, and it would probably fall on unwilling ears anyway. Instead, he patted Haley's shoulder. "He'll come around. Guys aren't all that bad."

"I know. Love doesn't stink for everyone." Haley grinned and twisted one braid around her finger. "For example, I think you and Lori will make a great couple."

"Shh!" Andy's grip tightened around the can, and the aluminum crackled. He lowered his head to her level. "You agreed to keep that a secret."

Haley shrugged. "No one's around. Besides, you can't keep it hidden forever—especially if you want a date for Valentine's Day. Eventually she'll figure out the gifts are from you."

"Not if you avoid being seen as we discussed." And unfortunately, not if Lori's current train of thought kept whistling toward Monny.

Andy squeezed the can harder, and a bubble of Coke blurped from the open tab. He had to find a way to show Lori—subtly, of course, so as not to scare her away—that the gifts were from him. The next present would have to be perfect, something romantic and meaningful—and, most importantly, something that would hint at his identity while not taking away the air of mystery. Somehow, it would do all of those things and leave him looking much more appealing than Monny.

He took another sip of Coke and felt the cold liquid trickle down his throat. *Right. And I'm the next Joe Montana.*

Lori secured the lid back on a two-liter bottle of Dr Pepper and slid the full plastic cup toward a young man with multiple tattoos on his arms. "Here you go."

"Thanks." He took the cup and smiled before leaving to mingle with the rest of the youth group. A few years ago, Lori would have seen someone like that—tattooed and pierced—on the streets and immediately cast judgment. But these kids had shown her that what was on the surface didn't always accurately reveal the heart.

She watched the tattooed guy meander through the crowd toward Andy, who greeted the young man by name and slung an arm around his thin shoulders in greeting. It seemed Andy was finally back in top form. The first half of his sermon she'd wondered if he was okay—he looked distracted, almost frustrated at times. But the longer he talked about the importance of friendship and fellowshipping together at church, the more involved he became, and eventually that determined spark lit his eyes once again. Now he interacted with the youth group as if he had nothing else on his mind.

Friendship—Andy's specialty. Lori supposed he was living proof of the age-old argument that a man and woman could be just friends and nothing else. She sighed. Story of her life. She'd sworn off dating after Jason cheated on her. Now that she finally felt a little more interest in getting out there again, her Mr. Right remained oblivious.

Lori shoved the two-liter across the counter to make room and leaned over, bracing her elbows against the worn Formica and wishing she could turn off her worries as fast as Andy seemed to during the sermon. Who was her secret admirer? Not Andy, as much as she wanted him to be. He didn't have a romantic bone in his body—and definitely not toward her, the girl he burped in front of during monthly movie nights at her town house. If Andy cared about impressing her, he would have done so long before now. They'd been friends for years, and he'd never shown even a flicker of interest. Lori learned months ago to quit trying before her heart got broken yet again.

All secret-admirer signs pointed to Monny. Earlier today, when she told Andy as much, she'd felt almost certain Monny was the culprit. But once she and Monny left for the day, he gave his usual goodbye wave and wink and disappeared into the back alley without a word about the flowers. Lori couldn't decide if she felt disappointed or relieved. Interest from a handsome Italian chef would definitely be a day-brightener, but in the overall picture, it didn't matter. She wouldn't date Monny even if he was her secret admirer. Despite his charm, dark good looks and delicious accent, he just wasn't Andy—silly, rumpled, prankster Andy, who could always make Lori laugh with a dumb joke and tell what she was thinking often before Lori even knew herself.

Lori traced her fingernail across the fading design on the countertop, and the rhythmic thumping of a dribbling basketball nearby punctuated her thoughts. Maybe she'd imagined the whole thing. The flowers and card were real enough, but maybe the secret-admirer concept wasn't. Just because the card was signed that way didn't mean someone was being serious. It could have even been a youth-group member playing a joke.

"Lori? You okay?" Haley stepped up to the counter and waved her hand in front of Lori's face. "You're totally somewhere else."

"No, I'm here. Just thinking." Lori straightened, then frowned as a movement across the gym caught her attention. Andy was staring at them, his face pale and drawn, his eyes wide. He stepped forward as if to approach them but was held back by a youth-group member demanding his attention. He looked back and forth between the kid and Lori before settling his gaze on the youth, the panicked expression only slightly fading.

Was Andy feeling sick again? She'd have to talk to him after the kids left and make sure he was okay. Lori turned her attention back to Haley. "What kind of drink do you want?"

"How about one that will give me enough guts to tell Jeremy I want to get back together?" She slumped over the countertop, mimicking Lori's previous position.

Lori smiled. "Trouble in teen paradise?"

"Something like that." Haley rolled her eyes.

"I think Coke should do the trick." Lori poured her a glass and slid it across the counter. "What's going on?"

"I was fine with our breakup, but after hearing Pastor

Andy's talk tonight on friendship, I realized that I miss him. Jeremy is—was—my best friend on top of being my boyfriend." Haley poked an ice cube with her pink-painted fingernail. "I guess I forgot that part when we started fighting and called it quits."

"He'll take you back."

"How can you be so sure?"

"Because he probably feels the exact same way." Lori gestured over Haley's shoulder. Jeremy stood alone near the stage, hands in his pockets and head hung low, as if studying his shoes. He shuffled his feet, looked over toward the kitchen where Haley stood, then down again.

Haley turned back to Lori. "What should I do?"

"You know what they say." Lori nudged the plate of leftover chocolate cookies closer to Haley. "The way to a man's heart…"

Haley plucked two cookies from the pile, hope lighting her eyes. "Thanks, Lori. Of course you would think of that, working at the Chocolate Gator and all. I bet—"

"Wait, how do you know where I work?" Lori interjected. That was odd. She hadn't told any of the youth-group kids yet. "I just started."

Haley's eyes widened to giant orbs. "Um, Pastor Andy mentioned it earlier. When I asked where the cookies came from." She snatched a napkin from the counter. "Gotta go. Thanks again." Then she whisked across the floor toward Jeremy, narrowly dodging a man rolling up the thick black cords from the sound table.

Lori tapped her finger against the half-empty bottle of Coke, watching Haley present her peace-offering dessert to Jeremy. He offered a tentative smile, and then they hugged and simultaneously bit into their cookies.

If only every relationship were that easy. Lori almost wished for the complicated days of high school. Wasn't growing up supposed to get easier? Yet now, the one man who seemed to show genuine interest in her remained a mystery and couldn't possibly be the man she wanted.

Lori nibbled on the edge of a cookie and relaxed as the chocolate melted in her mouth. She missed Gracie. Her best friend would know exactly what to say at a time like this, what to advise, how to cheer her up. They'd talked on the phone a few times since Gracie and Carter's wedding, but Lori didn't want to bug her friend on her honeymoon. Thanks to Carter's wealth from his old life of music-industry fame, they were able to take an extended vacation together and start their marriage off with month-long tans and all the seafood they could eat.

What would Gracie say if she were here? After sharing some chocolate, she'd probably tell Lori to step it up a notch. Dust off her flirting abilities that were stored on a high shelf after her nasty breakup with Jason and get back in the game. If someone was pursuing her, she should pursue right back, even if it wasn't Andy, aka Mr. Right.

Maybe Mr. Good Enough—whoever he was—would be better than nothing.

# *Chapter Six*

Lori looked up as the bell above the shop door jingled. A boy, maybe ten years old, came inside carrying a gift-wrapped box. He set it on the counter in front of her, scratched his nose and turned to leave.

"Wait!" Lori dropped the supplies catalog she'd been paging through and grabbed for the present. No card or tag. "Who is this from?"

The boy kept going, pausing once to hitch up his baggy jeans. "Don't know."

"What do you mean you don't know? How can you not know?"

He turned around at the door and shrugged. "I'm not supposed to say." He pushed at the handle, and the bell jingled again.

Lori reached over the counter as if she could stop him from across the room. "Wait, I…" Her eyes narrowed, and she smiled. "Want some chocolate?"

The door clicked shut as he made a beeline for the counter.

Lori triumphantly reached under the display and pulled out a caramel-crème chocolate. "Here. Now tell me what you know."

"Shmm laymie." Chocolate oozed around the sides of the boy's mouth as he chomped on the dessert.

"Excuse me?" Lori shoved a napkin toward him.

He swallowed twice. "Some lady. She said not to tell you who."

A woman? Lori frowned. Obviously it had to be another delivery person working on behalf of her secret admirer—someone she might recognize due to their request for anonymity. But why would Monny send someone to do the work when he could just wait for her to leave the room? She shoved her hair behind her ears and leaned forward. There had to be more to it. "You don't know her name?"

"Nope. She had blond hair."

"How old was she?"

The boy shrugged and crumpled the unused napkin in his hand. "Twenty? Maybe younger. Probably older, though. People think I look eight, but I turned eleven last month."

Lori rocked back on her heels. Great. A wasted chocolate out of her paycheck, and still no information other than the gift was delivered by someone who could fit the description of almost half the women in the city. "All right. Thanks anyway."

"Thanks for the chocolate, lady." He grinned, showing caramel stains on his teeth.

"Consider it a late birthday gift." Lori waited until the kid left before fingering the red ribbon around the box. Why didn't her admirer just mail the box? Maybe it contained something expensive, something they wanted to be sure arrived safely.

So they entrusted it to an eleven-year-old boy?

Lori shook her head. Only way to find out was to open it. She could do that now, then confront Monny about the gift when he returned from his break. He had to be her secret admirer—there were no other options. After sleeping on her emotional thoughts from last night's service, Lori decided that Mr. Good Enough wasn't good enough after all, and she'd rather be alone than lead someone on. Heartbreak, she knew from experience, wasn't fun for anyone. She would have to be gentle.

Lori's stomach fluttered in anticipation as she slid the bow off the package and ripped open the cardboard flaps. She rummaged through the piles of packing paper, fingers eagerly searching. Just because she might have to return the gifts after Monny confessed his love didn't mean she couldn't enjoy the process. Her hand hit something soft. With an expectant grin, Lori tugged the item free of the gift wrap.

A stuffed Hershey's Kiss.

A quick look inside the box confirmed there were a handful of the real chocolate pieces nestled in among the colored tissue—nothing more. A confused frown nestled between Lori's brows. They worked in an upscale chocolate boutique in the French Quarter, and Manny had sent candy she could have gotten from Wal-Mart? Granted, it was her favorite, but she expected more from someone who made exquisite chocolate every day.

Clutching the little stuffed toy in both hands, Lori turned with determination toward the kitchen. She'd have to help Monny out. Even if she wasn't interested in dating the handsome Italian, she could at least help him with a few pointers for his next love interest.

It was the least she could do after breaking his heart.

Andy strolled toward the Chocolate Gator, anticipation building in his stomach—and it wasn't about the chocolates he'd soon be consuming. No, in just a few minutes, he'd see Lori face-to-face, and she'd thank him for the gift he'd sent.

He picked up his step and whistled a little tune. A street artist nodded in greeting as he passed, and Andy paused long enough to toss a quarter into the open guitar case of a performing musician. He couldn't be happier—his idea was genius. After seeing the Hershey's Kisses, Lori would have to put two and two together and realize he was her admirer. After all, he was the one who kept the bowl of Kisses on his desk at work, the bowl she visited frequently. Who else supplied her with a constant stream of chocolate at the church? Plus, the gift was cute—borderline corny. Subtle, and yet obvious at the same time. In other words, perfect.

His breath tightened as he walked. Only two more storefronts and he'd be under the Chocolate Gator's pink-and-black-striped awning. Andy's stomach swished with nerves, and he paused to check his hair in the reflection of a store window. He really should get it cut, but he looked so young with his forehead showing. He swiped at a stubborn cowlick with his fingers.

Andy's cell rang, and his heart jumped like an old man caught dozing during church. Maybe it was Lori, calling to tell him she'd figured out his secret identity. With a smile, he flipped open the cell. "I was just heading to see you—"

"You'll have an awfully long swim if you do." The familiar deep voice of his friend Carter chuckled through the line.

"Carter!" Andy dropped onto a nearby bench. Andy's musician best friend had recently married Lori's friend Gracie. Andy liked to think he had a little something to do with the perfect match. After all, he and Carter were college roommates and Gracie had been a part of Andy's church long before Carter showed back up in her life. Andy grinned. "How's the sun and sand?"

"Both are pretty hot." A female voice chimed in on Carter's end of the line, and he laughed. "And so is my new wife, of course."

Andy snorted. "Don't make me hang up on you. Haven't ya'll had enough alone time yet?"

"Never. Marriage is the best, man. I highly recommend it."

"So does Pastor Mike." Andy quickly filled Carter in on what had transpired over the last week.

"Wow, no pressure, huh?" Carter clucked his tongue. "So who's the unlucky girl?"

"Funny."

"You know I've got to give you a hard time. You gave me enough flak about Gracie."

"How about some helpful advice? You can tease me after the wedding."

"Deal." Carter paused. "Wedding? So there *is* a girl?"

Andy immediately sobered. If he told Carter whom he had in mind, Gracie would know minutes after. Gracie was Lori's best friend. Her knowing Andy's feelings toward Lori would possibly help—or seriously hurt if she didn't approve. He swallowed. "Someone you know pretty well."

"Just spit it out, man. We're about to go on a glass-bottom boat ride." He whispered something to Gracie about tickets, then stopped short. "You didn't finally come to your senses about Lori, did you?"

Andy opened his mouth, then closed it. Had he been that obvious to everyone but himself in the last year or two?

"It's Lori, isn't it? She's the one!" Andy couldn't tell if Carter's voice held excitement or shock. Maybe both. He stood and began to pace the sidewalk, narrowly dodging a little boy on a skateboard. That would make sense—it was exactly how Andy felt, too.

"Hold on. Gracie wants to talk to you."

Andy's stomach rolled, and he gripped the cell tighter in his sweaty palm.

"Andy? Are you serious?" Gracie's melodic voice traveled from the Gulf as clearly as if she sat beside him. "You're interested in Lori?"

"Yes?" It came out more like a question, and he cleared his throat. "I mean, yes. I am."

She squealed so loudly he jerked the phone away from his ear, heart pounding louder than the guy playing the bongo drums on the corner. "It's about time!"

He dropped back onto the empty bench and exhaled. "Thanks, I think."

"How was your first date? I can't believe she hasn't called me!"

"There actually hasn't been one."

A pause hovered over the line. "She doesn't know how you feel, does she?"

"Not yet." He told her about the gifts he'd sent. "I was just on my way to see her at the shop, and I bet she'll have it figured out by the time I get there."

"Because of a Hershey's Kiss?" Gracie laughed. "Andy, it's a sweet thought, but Lori begs, borrows or buys chocolate from a dozen different people and places. I think you're going to have to be more obvious if you want to be discovered. Although it's pretty silly to keep up this secret-admirer facade in the first place, if you ask me."

"You don't think I should do it?"

"I just think you should give Lori a fair shot at accepting you for who you are. You might be surprised."

"Has she said something about me before?" Andy leaned forward and braced his elbows against his knees. The same skateboarding kid rolled back by, the wheels scraping loudly on the concrete. Andy turned his head to better hear Gracie's answer, anticipation hovering like a little child around a beignet.

"Well, no. Not exactly. But why the secrecy?"

Andy opened his mouth to explain, but Carter's muffled voice on the other end of the line interrupted. "Gracie, we're going to miss the tour if we don't leave now."

A scuffling sounded, as if Gracie had clamped her hand over the receiver. "Just a second, this is important." She returned to the phone. "Andy, we've got to go. Listen, just take it slowly, but don't be afraid to tell her what's in your heart, okay?"

"Okay." He said goodbye and disconnected the call. His agreement to Gracie's suggestion still lingered on his lips, but its meaning didn't settle in his gut. He knew what he was doing. There was no way Lori would be responsive to his stating right out that he had feelings for her. She'd be shocked—and not in a good way. They'd been close friends for so long now she'd probably never thought of him as anything other than her best friend. Even if Lori was mistaking Monny as her secret admirer, he had to keep it up a while longer and ease her into the concept of Andy being boyfriend material.

Make that husband material.

Lori slid a tray of chocolate-dipped marshmallows into the display case. She'd already popped a few into her mouth—taste-testing for the customer's sake, of course—and now she wanted to eat the whole pan. She needed fortification if she intended to confront Monny about being her secret admirer. She'd tried earlier in the afternoon, but he'd been intensely focused on icing a special-order cake, and she hadn't wanted to distract him. That'd just be one more thing she would mess up.

The bell tinkled, and Andy strolled inside. Lori's eyes widened. She couldn't talk to Monny about the gifts in front of Andy—Monny would be mortified when she turned him down. She had to get rid of Andy.

"Hey, there." She forced a smile as Andy approached the counter. Any other time she'd be glad to see her friend, but right now, all she could think about was getting the misunderstanding with Monny cleared up before he did something embarrassing—like confess his love in that smooth accent for all the store to hear.

"Hi. Just thought I'd drop by and see how things were going." Andy tapped the glass with his palms as he studied the contents of the display.

"They're going fine." Lori frowned, thoughts of her secret-admirer situation suddenly far away. "Why wouldn't they be?" Surely Andy wasn't dropping in to check on her *again,* was he? She was perfectly capable of running this store without him.

Well, mostly.

"I'm sure they are. I just had to ask. I mean, wanted to ask." Andy shook his head, and his hair flopped in his eyes.

"Well, the store is going great. So, how can I help you?" Lori straightened her shoulders and turned on her most professional voice. Andy needed to leave *now*—before she lost her chance to confront Monny, and before Andy angered her further with his lack of trust. Why did he even refer her to Bella if he didn't trust her to be a good manager?

Andy's eyes flickered with hurt at the dismissal. "Um, I guess two of the chocolate crocodiles should do it."

Lori quickly bagged his order and rang it up on the register. "Three dollars and seventy-five cents."

Andy slipped her a five-dollar bill. "Keep the change." His smile didn't quite meet his eyes this time, and Lori pushed back a wave of guilt. It was Andy's own fault for coming in here and checking up on her like he owned the place.

"See you later." Lori offered a little wave as she shut the register drawer. *Hurry up, before Monny gets involved in another cake.* Her opportunity was slipping, and Lori didn't know how much longer she could work with Monny without setting things straight between them.

Andy finally headed toward the door, devoid of his usual spark. "Right. See you." The door chimed on his way out, and Lori breathed a sigh of relief. One disaster averted.

But now Summer sat perched on her stool with her usual magazine, offering zero privacy for Lori and Monny's pending conversation.

"Summer, will you take out the trash, please? The can by the door is full." Lori glanced over her shoulder. "Summer? Summer!"

The younger girl jerked her iPod earphones to her neck and blinked twice. "You don't have to shout."

"The trash." Lori closed her eyes briefly and then pointed toward the can. "Please." She waited until Summer was occupied with the rustling garbage bag, then peeked through the window of the kitchen door. Monny had finished the cake and was dumping dirty pots in the industrial-size sink.

"Summer, why don't you go load the dishwasher next? And

while you're back there, please ask Monny to come out here."
Perfect. Now she could have Monny's undivided attention, and
Summer would be occupied—and productive.

Without a word, Summer tucked the edges of the new garbage bag around the wastebasket and disappeared through the
swinging door. Lori ran her fingers through her hair and
straightened her pink top. Not that it really mattered. Monny
apparently liked her the way she was, or he wouldn't have
started sending her gifts—again, not that it mattered. Tempting
as it was to date Monny to avoid being alone, she couldn't do
that to her heart. She and Monny had to stay just friends, even
if he was infatuated with her.

Monny stepped through the kitchen doorway. "Yes, *mi cara?*
You wanted to see me?" He stopped in front of her, close
enough she could smell the strawberry crème dotting his apron.

"I just… I…" The words dangled off her lips, teasing them
both. He looked so sweet standing there with a smile, calling her
"my dear," that she almost couldn't bring herself to say anything.
She coughed and tried again. "I wanted to say thank you."

"*Prego.* But for what?"

"For the gifts." Lori gestured toward the flower bouquet. The
petals were starting to dry and brown, but the overall arrangement still brightened the counter display.

Monny's dark eyebrows meshed into one, and he shook his
head. "I don't understand."

"You're my secret admirer. I'm sorry that I figured it out so
fast. You might not have been ready." Lori took a deep breath
and offered what she hoped came across as a compassionate
smile. "But I'm not ready, either. To date, that is. I appreciate
the gifts, but a relationship just isn't smart. We're coworkers,
and we should keep things professional." *Not to mention I'm
in love with someone else.*

There. Now the truth was out in the open, dancing in the
space between them just like the dust particles waltzing their

way through the sunbeams on the shop floor. Relief drooped Lori's shoulders. She'd done it, taken the high road, despite the fact that she had no prospects for Valentine's Day or the future beyond and no hopes of acquiring any.

Monny edged away from her, both hands held up in a defensive gesture. "I'm sorry, *mi cara*, I don't know what you're talking about."

Lori stepped forward. "Of course you do. The flowers and the chocolate Kisses. I really appreciate the gifts, but—"

"I did not send them." Monny shrugged one shoulder and grinned. "I have a fiancée back home in Italy."

# Chapter Seven

Lori sat in the darkened shop at the counter, heels tucked against the top rung of the stool, listlessly fingering her wilting bouquet. The flowers drooped as if sensing her feelings of rejection, their petals browning around the edges in sympathy as her dreams for the future withered.

She'd never been so embarrassed in her life. Not even when she tripped in new high heels and sprawled across the stage at the church a few months back. Or even that time she spilled gumbo down the front of a paying customer at the fundraiser last year for the aquarium. No, this was worse—complete and utter humiliation.

*I have a fiancée.* Monny's words churned over and over in her mind like mixer beaters set on high speed. How many shades of red had she turned? He must think she was a moron. A moron who couldn't bake, a moron who could barely handle managing a store that should practically run itself, and even worse—a moron who was so desperate for love she imagined attention from engaged coworkers.

With a groan, Lori dropped her forehead to her hands. How could she face Monny tomorrow? Suddenly his departure to Italy couldn't come fast enough.

Her pro/con list wrinkled under her elbows, and she lifted her eyes enough to peer at the paper she'd prepared a few days prior. Pros for her secret admirer being Monny filled the left side of the sheet, a few lines down. Entries included *It would be nice to be taken on a date now and then* and *Someone is better than no one.* Cons for the same took up many lines more on the right side. *Long-distance relationships are hard.* And most importantly—*He's not Andy.*

She should add one more item to the con column: *He's not interested.*

A scuffling noise sounded behind her, and Lori jerked. She'd already locked up the store. Had someone broken in? She whirled around on the stool just in time to see Summer flicking on the light switch.

"Summer! What are you doing here?" Lori pressed one hand to the heart threatening to burst through her thin purple sweater.

"I work here." Summer arched a pierced eyebrow. "Remember?"

"I meant after hours. Do you have a key?"

"The kitchen door was unlocked."

Lori briefly closed her eyes. Monny must have forgotten to lock it after he left for the night. No wonder—he probably ran out as fast as he could. And to think she started the conversation with the intention of rejecting *him.*

"I left my iPod." Summer moved to the counter beside Lori and picked up the shiny silver player from under the register. "Besides, the better question is, why are you sitting here in the dark?" She did a double take at Lori's tearstained face. "Are you okay?"

"I'm fine." Lori wiped her eyes and winced at the mascara darkening her fingertips. Great. She probably looked as silly as she felt.

"Right—and I'm the next Rachael Ray." Summer rolled her eyes. "Listen, if you don't want to talk, whatever. But don't lie." She waited a beat. "I'm really tired of liars."

"Me, too." Lori sighed. Maybe she and Summer had more in common than Lori first thought, despite the silver stud in the younger girl's nose and the butterfly tattoo adorning her wrist. Hadn't the youth group at the church taught her that much? Besides, at this point Lori had nothing to lose. Maybe telling Summer about her embarrassment would lift the burden a little. "I just made a huge mistake."

"Who hasn't?" Summer shrugged and leaned against the counter, bracing her elbows against the top.

"A really embarrassing mistake."

"Again, who hasn't?" Summer slipped her iPod into the pocket of her jeans. "You're starting to bore me, Boss." She winked, lightening the harsh words, and suddenly Lori couldn't wait to pour out her story.

When she finished, Summer nodded slowly. "You were right."

"About what?" Lori frowned.

"That was a really huge, really embarrassing mistake."

Lori laughed despite the fact that nothing had changed. "Told you." Amazing how much better she felt wallowing with someone instead of alone.

"Here." Summer stretched over and hit a few keys on the register. The drawer popped open, and she removed the key to the glass display at their knees. "You need chocolate."

"I can't—I mean, that's not ours to take," Lori protested in vain as Summer slid open the case and plucked two cherry bonbons from a lace doily.

"Take it out of my paycheck, Boss, if it's that big a deal." Summer closed the door, handed Lori the dessert and laid the key back on the register.

Lori stared at the piece in her hand, made a mental note to pay for it the next day and popped the chocolate into her mouth. She chewed slowly, closing her eyes and letting the flavors dissolve on her tongue. "Wow, that's good."

"You hadn't had one yet?"

Lori shook her head, mouth full of cherry crème.

Summer made a *tsk* noise. "They're Monny's specialty."

The candy dried in her mouth, and Lori had to force herself to swallow. "Great."

"The man can cook. Might be a lousy coworker, leading you on the way he did, but he can cook."

"You really think he led me on? I didn't imagine all that?" Hope tottered at the edges of Lori's heart. Maybe she hadn't been desperate after all—maybe she'd been deceived instead of stupid.

Summer tilted her head to one side and bit into the second half of her bonbon. "Not *all* of it."

"But some."

"Yes, some."

They chewed in silence.

"I don't understand. He flirted with me." Lori shifted on her stool, feeling even more ridiculous for discussing her love life with a college-aged stranger. Somehow, though, Summer seemed like the last person who'd pass judgment. "You noticed it, right?"

"Sure I did. But did *you* not notice him calling most of the women customers 'my dear' and flashing that Italian smile all over the place?"

No. Lori fought the urge to grab another piece of chocolate. "I'm a bigger dork than I thought."

"Don't feel bad. It could have happened to anyone." Summer brushed her hands on her back pockets. "Guys like Monny are just that way. They don't think about how we interpret things. There's a dude in my psych class who did the same thing to my best friend. Chatted her up like he was interested, then went out with someone else in the class days later."

"But Monny has a fiancée. That's not a date—that's a serious commitment." But even as the words left her lips, Lori realized she'd made his flirtations into something more than he intended. She was so desperate to get Andy to notice her she'd invented a fill-in for Mr. Right in her own mind.

Poor Monny.

Lori scowled at the dying flower bouquet. Probably the heat from the kitchen had wilted them faster than usual. It figured that she couldn't even enjoy them longer. But now their presence was more annoying than pleasant. If it hadn't been for those gifts arriving, she would have never taken things so far in her mind with Monny. But if not him, then who? The bouquet was real. So was the silly little Hershey's Kiss stuffed in her purse under the counter. Speaking of which, she should probably burn the thing. Every time she saw it, she'd remember the achingly awkward moment when Monny had looked at her with stark confusion in his eyes. Her face flamed with the memory.

"Forget about Monny. He won't hold it against you. It's embarrassing, but at least you were turning him down and not throwing yourself at him." Summer touched the brittle petals of the arrangement, wincing as one broke off onto the counter.

True. If Lori had been accepting Monny's offer—well, imaginary offer—she would have been a lot more embarrassed.

"You should focus on whoever out there *is* your secret admirer. It's still pretty cool to have one." Summer shrugged.

"You're right." Lori stood, the legs of the stool screeching against the tile floor. The awkward moment of the past was over, and someone out there actually did have a thing for her. She could still enjoy the gifts even if she didn't intend on reciprocating. The mystery of "what if" was pretty romantic—and for a girl destined to be alone like her, it was probably as good as it was going to get.

One thing was certain: she'd be absolutely positive next time before accusing any more unsuspecting men of loving her.

Summer slapped her palm against the countertop. "No more moping around. I think we should do a little detective work and try to figure out who's behind the gifts. What do you say?"

Lori picked up the display key Summer had left on the register and shot her new friend a grin. "I say, who wants more chocolate?"

\* \* \*

His genius plan apparently wasn't quite as genius as he first imagined.

Andy tossed the basketball toward the goal at the end of the gym. It bounced off the rim—figured. Sort of like it figured Lori hadn't called yet. And why should she—because he sent her a stuffed piece of candy and some chocolate? If she believed her secret admirer to be that foreign baker, he might as well give up now. Who was Andy compared to a suave Italian who could whip up her dream dessert in minutes? No wonder she was practically shoving him out the door when he stopped by. She wanted to be alone with the chef.

He shot again and missed. Definitely not on his game today.

"It's all in the wrist, Pastor." Jeremy held out his hands for the ball. "Watch a pro."

Andy bounced the ball across the wooden floor to him, and Jeremy easily nailed a three-pointer. "Come on now—I thought you were a football player."

"I'm an *athlete*." Jeremy dribbled twice before shooting again. "We're naturals at all sports."

"My mistake." Andy shot and missed a second time. "I'm too old for this." And distracted. But that was hardly an excuse not to keep up with a high-schooler—though Jeremy did have at least four inches on him.

Andy checked the ball back to him, and Jeremy shot again. Nothing but net.

"Nah, you're not too old." Jeremy spun the ball on the tip of his finger. "Maybe too old for football. Wouldn't want you to get hurt, Pastor." He grinned.

"Very funny." Andy pulled one arm in a stretch over his head. Goofing around in the gym with one of his youth-group members was much better than sulking in his office, staring at the budget proposal he'd yet to complete and wondering what to do next about Lori.

Yet thoughts of her still managed to creep into his mind. She obviously hadn't linked him to the Hershey's Kisses, and the more he thought about it, the more he realized Gracie was right. Too subtle. He didn't want to be so obvious with his gifts that Lori felt rushed into a relationship with him, but at the same time, he had to somehow let her know the giver wasn't Monny. At this point, he was almost tempted to get tips from the guy. Weren't Europeans all naturally romantic? Women thought so, anyway—and romance was definitely not Andy's specialty.

Yet something about Lori made him want to try.

Plus, Andy was running out of time. Last Sunday, Pastor Mike had casually mentioned setting Andy up with his niece. There was no way he would even consider getting involved with someone in the senior staff's family. Talk about a disaster waiting to happen.

No, the sooner he could show the staff he was taking their request seriously and find his own girlfriend, the better—for the church and for the youth group, not to mention for his own sanity. It was hard to devote his full energy to the kids with this kind of pressure hanging over his head like a cloud over a parade. In this case, the parade was his life—and Andy was getting a little tired of the rain.

The basketball whizzed past his head, and Andy blinked. "Hey!"

"Focus is key in sports, Pastor." Jeremy wiped his face with the neck of his jersey. "Or at least that's what Coach says."

Andy jogged to retrieve the ball. "Your coach is right."

"Then where's your head?"

Nowhere that he could share. The last thing Andy needed was the youth group rallying for him and Lori to get together. Her rejection would be hard enough to take without an audience. Andy shrugged and aimed for the backboard.

"You're thinking about Lori, aren't you?"

The ball slipped from his fingers and fell to the floor. *"What?"*

"Haley told me." Jeremy scooped up the abandoned ball and tucked it under his arm.

"She promised she wouldn't tell." Andy rammed his fingers against his pulsing temples as frustration clouded his vision. He couldn't believe Haley had gone against her word like that. He shouldn't have trusted her with something so personal. What if Lori found out sooner than he intended? Panic gripped his stomach, and he swallowed the nerves creeping up his throat.

"Don't worry, when Haley got to the part about promising to keep it a secret, I got mad at her for telling me. But she said boyfriends didn't count as *anyone*." Jeremy rolled his eyes. "Women."

No kidding. Now what was he going to do?

"I won't say anything, Pastor. Relationships are private, I get that. Haley tells enough people about our business." Jeremy sighed. "Though I guess that's what I get for being in love with a high-school kid."

Andy bit back the retort forming about Jeremy being a high-school kid himself. "I'd appreciate your keeping it quiet. You don't really understand what all is at stake here."

"Hey, it's about a woman, Pastor. I think I understand as much as any guy can." Jeremy tossed him the ball and laughed.

Andy clamped his sweaty palms around the ball's hard, bumpy surface. Pointless to argue—he couldn't exactly tell Jeremy about the senior pastor's request. Now Andy had a second clock ticking a warning in his ears. What if it was too late? Word was spreading, and since she hadn't called, Lori obviously wasn't ready to reciprocate his feelings—even though she seemed more than willing to do so with Monny's.

The gym seemed to close in on Andy, and he shook the damp hair out of his eyes. He had to step it up a notch. Maybe send gifts more often, give better hints. If his competition was a foreign charmer with really great hair, then romance was going to be key. It was all in the details.

And no one knew Lori better than he did.

Andy drew a deep breath and lobbed the basketball toward the net. *Swish.*

Maybe he still had a chance after all.

## Chapter Eight

"**I**'m never dating again."

"Don't give up. It's only been a few days—we'll figure out who your mystery man is. Be patient. I'll come up with something." Summer looked up from rummaging through a bargain bin of purses. "And here I thought I was negative."

Lori checked the price on the bottom of a pink high-heeled pump and winced before setting it back on the shelf. "I'm not negative. I'm realistic. And while we're waiting to figure it out, Monny's avoiding me like I have Ebola or something."

"He's probably trying not to give you the wrong idea again." Summer brushed her fingers against a purple feather boa that was part of a display.

"Maybe I should talk to Monny." Lori sighed. "I don't want work to be awkward because of a silly misunderstanding."

"When does he go back to Italy?"

"Not for a few months."

"Bummer." Summer scowled at a pair of boots. "Why did you bring me here again? This place is too girlie. Nothing but shoes and purses."

"Exactly. You need some color in your life." Lori handed her a pink purse. "Here. Valentine's Day is in two weeks. This would be great."

Summer ducked away from the bag as if it were going to consume her. "No way! I don't do pink. And I definitely don't do Valentine's Day."

"You need to do something other than black. You come across so hard and unapproachable."

"Thanks, Boss."

"You know what I mean." Lori dropped the pink tote and snagged a gold purse with blue stitching from the same bin. "What about this one?"

Summer's eyebrows knitted together, but she didn't run away. "Better." She looped the purse over her shoulder and stood beside the store's full-length mirror. "What do you think?"

"Perfect. Picks up the glint in your eyebrow ring."

Summer laughed and threw the purse at Lori. "Forget it."

"Maybe this isn't your kind of store after all." A pair of black-and-white polka-dot stilettos caught Lori's eye across the store. "But it's definitely mine."

"You could easily run a shop like this."

Lori picked up the polka-dotted sandal on display and searched the pile of boxes for her size. "I used to want to."

"Used to? Has working at the Chocolate Gator changed your mind?"

Lori tugged a size-nine box free from the stack and sat down to try them on. "It's made me realize I'm not cut out for managing."

Summer leaned against the shelf of shoes and scoffed. "Whatever. You figured out the coffee machine finally."

"Most days, anyway." Lori blew a wisp of hair out of her eyes and held up her foot to admire the sandal. "But it's more than the coffee machine. The customers haven't warmed up to me yet. I can't bake, and I don't know how many things I burned or messed up in the last two weeks."

"So baking isn't your forte. Big whoop." Summer planted one hand against her jeans-clad hip, her black fingernails standing out against the bleach-washed denim. "Who says you have to open a bakery? You're a shoe girl anyway."

"How'd you know?"

"Besides the fact that you've worn uncomfortable heels every day to work and currently are up to your elbows in shoe boxes?"

"Yeah, besides that."

"And the fact that your purse has matched your shoes in some form every day?"

"Maybe it *is* a little obvious."

"And—"

"Okay, okay, I get it!" Lori slid the sandal off her foot and stuck it back inside its cardboard home. "But wearing shoes doesn't make me qualified to open a shoe store. Besides, I'd never have the money to do that."

Summer rolled her eyes. "It's called going to a bank."

"Banks like a little thing called good credit. Of which I have very little due to maxed-out credit cards and a few late payments." Lori pressed her lips together. It was her own fault. She'd done well enough at the aquarium the last few years but had grown bored. She wanted something new and exciting, an adventure. She wanted to be spontaneous and see what the world had to offer. So she got wind of a receptionist opening at a big law firm uptown, had a successful interview, gave two weeks' notice, and voilà—unemployed. She'd been living off her credit card before going to work for Andy's aunt, and even now, she still didn't have a permanent job. Once Bella returned from Shreveport, she'd take over, and Lori would be back to searching the classifieds.

While her dreams of opening her own boutique dwindled faster than her savings account.

"I'm just saying I think you could do it." Summer held up a pair of red ballet flats and grimaced. "Even if you did sell stuff like this."

Lori slid her feet into her own shoes and put the red flats and the polka-dotted heels back on the shelf. "Well, thanks for your vote of confidence, but I can't even begin to think about opening my own store if I can't handle running the Chocolate Gator."

They headed toward the shop doors. Why was everything going wrong at Bella's store? Lori had successfully managed the gift shop at the Aquarium of the Americas and never had any trouble. In hindsight, she should have stayed there. But there was no advancement in that position, no career-ladder climbing. Just stocking and ordering and standing behind a counter all day.

If she was destined to be alone all her life, she wanted to at least have a successful, enjoyable career.

Summer pushed open the glass door, and Lori followed, casting one last look over her shoulder at the shoes she left behind. She wasn't about to waste her first paycheck on more footwear—even if they were on sale. Food came first.

"Can we swing back by the shop before you go home?" Summer squinted against the fading winter sun and shaded her eyes with her hand.

"Sure. Did you forget something?"

"My jacket. Since the shop is closed tomorrow, I might need it."

"No problem."

The store was shut up tight for the coming weekend. Lori was glad Bella kept the shop closed on Sunday. She'd hate to miss church tomorrow because of work. She slid her key into the lock and flipped the light switch.

Summer edged past Lori and snagged her jacket from behind the counter. "Wow, it's cold back here." She shivered.

"It feels fine by the door." Lori stepped farther into the shop with a frown. "That's weird. The heater should have been on all day."

Summer backed toward the kitchen. "It's even worse over

here." She slipped her arms into her jacket sleeves and pushed open the swinging kitchen door. "Uh-oh."

Lori's heart fell into her stomach. "What now?" She rushed after Summer and stopped short in the doorway to the kitchen. The commercial-sized freezer door hung wide open—exactly what it had probably done for the last several hours that they'd been gone to dinner and shopping.

Summer winced. "Guess there goes our next run of supplies."

Lori couldn't look away from the melting mess inside the freezer. *Guess there goes my job.*

Andy caught Lori's sleeve as she exited the pew in front of him. "Hey, there."

Lori looked up in surprise, then smiled. Andy's stomach flickered at the response, until he noticed her puffy eyes. His own smile faded. "You okay?"

"Didn't get much sleep last night, that's all." Her soft words were almost swallowed by the organ's closing chords.

"Too much chocolate before bed?" Andy crossed his arms over his chest, hoping to hide the fact that his heart threatened to leap from his button-down and go hopping across the pew into Lori's arms.

She groaned. "Don't even mention chocolate."

He pressed his hand to Lori's forehead. "You *are* sick, aren't you?"

She ducked away with a short laugh. "Just a little mishap at the store. Everything's fine."

Andy braced himself for the bad news he'd have to pass on to Bella. "What happened?" He really wanted Lori to succeed at this job, not only because he had referred her, but because Lori needed this. She'd been down since leaving the aquarium, and a career pick-me-up was definitely in order. Whatever had happened, it must have been pretty bad to keep her up all night. No wonder her head had kept drooping during the church service.

Lori's expression stiffened along with her shoulders. "Nothing happened. I mean, nothing I can't handle."

"I never doubted that." Andy's grin did little to ease the tension lines in her face, and his stomach flickered again, this time out of concern. "Come on, tell me."

She averted her eyes. "I found out the other day that Monny wasn't my secret admirer after all."

Andy's breath whooshed from his body in one triumphant release. "You did?" He struggled to keep his exuberant grin toned to a more natural response. Forget whatever happened at the store—this was great news. One less obstacle between him and Lori. Then reality slammed Andy with a cross-punch. Was the reason behind her lack of pep today disappointment over Monny instead of whatever had gone wrong at the shop? If so, then even with the truth revealed, Andy might still have some competition from the Italian chef. He instantly sobered. It looked as if Lori's ban on dating had been lifted—but not to Andy's advantage if she was interested in some other guy.

"Yeah, I did." Lori still wouldn't look at him, and she seemed ready to bolt from the pew at any minute. She'd had that same distant look last time he stopped by the store.

Andy's mouth dried. Somehow, he had to keep her here. "Do you want to grab some lunch and talk?" Not that he wanted her to cry on his shoulder about Monny, but being with Lori in any regard was better than not being with her. Besides, he might be able to pry out of her the details of what happened at the store that was so bad. Bella would need to know.

"No. I told you, everything is fine." Lori stepped aside to let an elderly gentleman exit the pew, then cradled her Bible in her arms. She stared down at the floor.

Andy lowered his head, trying to catch her gaze. "I feel like we haven't talked in forever. Are you sure you're not hungry?"

"It's not personal. The store is keeping me really busy,

that's all." She blew a wisp of her hair out of her face. Her smile looked tired and forced. "I'm just going to go home and take a nap."

He opened his mouth, then closed it. Pushing would probably make things worse. He stepped out of the aisle so she could move past him. "Are we still on for movie night this Friday?"

Lori hesitated.

"I know Carter and Gracie are gone this month and can't join us as usual, but come on. It's tradition." He smiled, hoping his plea didn't sound as pathetic to her as it did to him.

After an eternity, Lori nodded. "Sure. I'll bring the chocolate."

"I'll bring the popcorn."

"Sounds good." She edged another step toward the door, obviously wanting to leave.

Andy held up his hand in a wave, fighting the urge to reach for her and try to hug away her problems. "See you Friday, then."

He hesitated before following Lori up the aisle, not wanting to crowd her space. A firm grip on his arm stopped Andy midstride, and he turned to see Pastor Mike wearing a tense smile.

"Mornin', Pastor. Great sermon today." Andy smiled back, but Mike's expression didn't change.

"Thank you. It seemed to be received well." The pastor's eyes were directed over Andy's shoulder, and he had yet to release Andy's arm. "Listen, son, I'm not trying to pry, but have you considered my request any further?"

"Of course." Andy nodded respectfully, even though a thousand knots tied simultaneously in his stomach. A second talk already? The pressure on the church must be worse than Andy first imagined if Pastor Mike was stooping to this level of confrontation. Andy swallowed. It wasn't his fault Lori had yet to notice his intentions. He was trying all he knew to try. If he blurted his feelings spontaneously, Lori would bolt—much like she'd just done.

"I know this marriage business is tricky, but son, if you don't get serious about finding a bride, I'm not sure how much longer I can hold off the board." Pastor's Mike's voice lowered. "They're on me constantly with phone calls from parents. Our recent drop in youth-group numbers is partially because of this. Families are concerned for their kids ever since that scandal across town."

Andy's mind whirled. He knew he'd seen a drop in attendance lately, but he'd chalked it up to a winter slump. Summer was always a busier time of year, as there were more events offered. "Are you sure they aren't paranoid, Pastor? We have the spring retreat coming up, and it's always a hit. I'm sure attendance will—"

"I'm just telling you what I know," Pastor Mike interrupted with a firm clap on Andy's shoulder. "Keep up that effort, all right? Even an engagement would hold them awhile."

Andy nearly choked at the idea of proposing to Lori this soon. She'd probably laugh in his face and assume it was yet another one of his many jokes. Andy's throat tightened, and he sputtered a dispute.

Pastor Mike stopped his effort with a raised hand. "I realize you're doing all you can and that this kind of thing takes time. I know that. Others, however…" Pastor Mike's voice trailed off, and the meaning of the unspoken words struck Andy with numbing clarity.

He managed to pat Pastor Mike's back in return. "Yes, sir."

The pastor slipped up the aisle. Andy followed slowly, nodding at parishioners crowding the front doors in their exit and hoping his inner turmoil didn't show on his face. Which of the congregation members had complained to the senior staff about his single status? Which smiling face had gone behind his back out of fear instead of trusting his heart?

More importantly, which one started this snowball with Lori that was rapidly turning into an avalanche?

\* \* \*

Lori tucked the afghan over her shoulders and nestled her plate in her lap. Her ignored stomach started growling as soon as she arrived home. No wonder—she'd skipped dinner last night and breakfast this morning. Emotionally beating herself up tended to distract her from food. How could she have left the freezer door open so carelessly when she'd left for the day? There was no telling yet how much money she had cost the shop in supplies. She'd have to reorder first thing in the morning and hope they could do a rush delivery. That'd be an additional fee.

She bit into a chip, barely tasting as she crunched. The cost of her negligence was adding up.

Andy's pestering after church hadn't helped matters. That's why Lori had dodged the subject of her management failure by telling him about Monny. She couldn't exactly tell Andy she was ruining his aunt's store. It was bad enough he popped in every few days to check on her. He was one of her best friends—he should believe in her.

Though after this freezer problem, she wouldn't blame him if he didn't.

Her living room, normally cozy and homey, suddenly felt empty. Lori spoke into the silence. "God, I keep screwing things up. I never had any trouble running the gift shop at the aquarium. Are You trying to tell me I'm not cut out for this or for my own business? Are my dreams not in line with Your plans?"

She dropped her sandwich back on the plate. God obviously didn't want her in a relationship—not since the incident with Jason and her embarrassment with Monny, and definitely not after Andy had been her friend for years without interest in anything more. Now it seemed God didn't want her to have a career, either. What was she doing wrong?

What was wrong with her?

Lori bowed her head over her lunch. "God, a sign would be nice. Just some sort of direction, please."

She looked up, half expecting a neon arrow to flash across her den even though she knew better. But the room remained dim and cold. The only light shone from the floor lamp behind her, casting her silhouette across the coffee table.

Even her shadow was lonely.

## Chapter Nine

"A fishing lure?" Summer stopped sweeping and stared incredulously at the gift in Lori's hand.

"Apparently I've *lured* him in." Lori held up the accompanying card and couldn't help but grin. Her secret admirer was getting creative. The brightly colored box waiting at the front door of the shop Tuesday morning almost made her forget how she'd shut the store down Monday.

"Wow, that's the corniest thing I've ever heard."

"Corny. But sweet." Lori hung the neon feathered lure from a thumbtack on the bulletin board near the register. Flowers, stuffed animals, candy and now fish bait. What would her secret admirer think of next? More importantly, when would he reveal himself?

Summer shook the broom handle at Lori. "With that sense of humor, he's either a complete dork or Prince Charming."

"I still can't completely shake the idea of the gifts being a prank—especially after I was mistaken about Monny." Lori bit her lower lip and glanced over her shoulder toward the kitchen window, where Monny hummed as he finished preparing the morning's pastries. Thankfully things hadn't been too awkward between the two of them since last week's embarrassing mishap. The subject was definitely taboo, though—they kept their conversation to shop-related issues only. Lori missed the easy camaraderie they shared when she first started work. Monny was a charmer and a fun friend. No wonder he flirted so much—Lori was beginning to believe he had no choice. It seemed to leak out of his pores.

"That would be one elaborate prank. No, I think it's for real." Summer leaned her weight against the broom handle and paused. "Maybe S.A. has a plan in mind and will reveal himself when the time is right."

"S.A.?"

"Secret Admirer."

Lori sighed. "Well, S.A. better hurry. Because the idea of a complete stranger sending secret messages is a little unnerving."

"Maybe it's someone from your church."

"I only have friends there. It just doesn't make sense." Lori brushed the feathered lure with her fingers and watched it dangle on the thumbtack. "Even our singles group is practically nonexistent."

"So what if it is a stranger? Big deal." Summer shrugged.

Lori nibbled on her bottom lip. "That's true. People meet each other all the time off the Internet, and that works out, right?"

"Right." Summer tilted her head. "Then again, people also get murdered that way."

"You're so encouraging."

"Which part of me broadcasts encouragement, exactly?" Summer stepped away from the broom and gestured at her body with one arm. Head-to-toe black clothes. Silver piercings. Blond hair piled on top of her head in various knots.

Lori crossed her arms over her chest and squared off with Summer. "I see right through all that. I know you've got a heart of gold somewhere underneath all that metal and ink."

"Whatever, Boss. Just because I went shoe shopping with you doesn't mean I'm getting all soft." Summer grinned, jammed her iPod buds back in her ears and resumed sweeping.

Lori shook her head with a laugh and began stacking several chocolate bars on top of each other in a pyramid. Despite her claim, Summer had changed toward Lori in the past several days—all because Lori confided in her and made Summer feel needed. Lori had seen it a thousand times with the teens at the church—show a little interest, trust them with yourself and they opened right up. Lori might not know how to have a romantic relationship, but she knew how to be a friend.

Apparently that was her whole problem with Andy in the first place.

Andy signed his name at the bottom of the budget proposal and slid it across his desk with a satisfied sigh. Finally. One thing crossed off his never-ending to-do list. Now that the overdue budget proposal was ready to turn in, he could concentrate on the spring retreat for the youth group. This year it had to be a success or his job would really be at stake. Andy still needed to find a speaker—and the event was in less than two months.

His mind definitely wasn't where it should be. The church staff thought being single was a distraction? He scoffed. Wooing a woman was a distraction—not to mention hard.

The added pressure from the staff certainly wasn't helping. He was tempted to lock his office door to prevent Pastor Mike stopping by with another "suggestion."

Andy tapped his pen against one hand and stared out the window. A mild winter breeze drifted through the open pane and rustled the edges of his desktop calendar. Dried, dead leaves still clung stubbornly to the branches of the trees outside, testifying that autumn had passed and winter was attempting the same. All too soon, winter would turn to spring and those same trees would blossom with fresh life. One more season on its way out, one more season on its way in.

One more season spent alone.

A knock sounded on his open office door. Pastor Mike once

again stood in the frame like a bad case of déjà vu. Andy swallowed and gestured for him to come inside. Hopefully this impromptu visit wouldn't carry as big a shock as the last two. He mentally braced himself.

"I can't even see your desk for all the paperwork." Mike settled into a chair opposite Andy. "You should tell your boss you need a raise." He winked.

"Hey, Boss, I need a raise." Andy grinned.

"Take it to the board."

"Never mind."

Mike laughed. "How's that youth retreat coming along?"

Andy glanced at his paper-strewn desk and winced. "Slowly."

"It'll work out. You always pull something out of your hat." Mike steepled his fingers under his chin. "Speaking of, have you given any more thought to our previous discussion?"

It'd only been two days since the last discussion. Fighting a grimace, Andy plastered what he hoped was a casual smile across his face. "I have, actually. I've been working on a project of sorts."

"Project," Mike repeated slowly. He grinned. "Does the lady in question know she's being referred to in such a manner?"

The lady in question didn't even seem to want to talk to him lately, much less care about how she was referenced, but that wasn't worth mentioning right now. Andy shook his head. "We're getting there."

"I see."

No, he didn't, but again, not worth mentioning. Andy glanced at the framed photo on his desk of Lori and the rest of his youth-group volunteers, then away. He didn't want to tell the pastor who he had in his sights—not until Lori was acting more like her old self and Andy could determine if he actually had a chance.

Mike leaned forward. "In the meantime, have you considered meeting my niece?"

Andy shifted in his chair. He couldn't lie. But he hadn't considered dating her, and wouldn't. How could he make that sound anything but offensive? Andy swallowed. "I, uh…"

Lori appeared in the hallway at his open office door, all smiles and shiny hair, and he suddenly lost the ability to speak. She lifted her hand to knock, then stepped backward at seeing Pastor Mike. "Sorry to interrupt, I was just—"

"No, no, come on in." Mike stood and offered his seat to Lori. "Andy, we'll finish our chat later."

He had no doubt about that. Andy nodded, glad his flipping stomach couldn't show on the outside. He took a deep breath to steady his sudden nerves.

Lori took the chair Mike vacated and plunked her purple bag in her lap. "What was that all about?"

"Nothing. Just church business." Andy cleared his throat. It wasn't a lie. Unfortunately, his private life had somehow managed to become just that. They sure didn't teach these things in seminary. He gestured toward the bowl of candy on his desk. "Want a Kiss?"

Lori's eyes widened.

"Chocolate." He nudged the bowl closer to her, heart stammering. He mentally banged his head against his desk. *Idiot, idiot, idiot.* And the church staff wondered why this whole wife-courting thing was taking him so long. Maybe if he videotaped his pathetic efforts, they'd take pity on him.

"Sure." Lori reached over and snagged a piece of silver-wrapped candy. She opened it slowly. "We need to talk."

The back flips inside Andy's stomach twisted into a conga line. "We do?" He knew they did, of course, but were they finally on the same page at the same time? It seemed too good to be true. Maybe she had finally put together the Hershey's Kiss gift after seeing the candy on his desk.

"Yes." Lori tossed her hair over her shoulder and released a slow breath. "I really should have asked you this sooner."

Andy braced his elbows against his desk and steeled his

mind. This was it. She'd figured out the gifts were from him and was going to ask to confirm it. His heart pounded an erratic rhythm, and blood pulsed in his temples. He sucked in a lungful of air. "Go ahead."

Lori plucked at a loose thread on her purse. Nervous? Maybe she felt the same way he did after all. Maybe the gifts weren't a bad idea and he should have taken Gracie's advice and told Lori how he felt from the start. Maybe—

"Do you need me to work the spring retreat in April?"

Andy's jaw slacked, and he stared unseeing across his desk. Her words beat against his brain until finally comprehended. She wanted to talk about the upcoming youth event. Not secret gifts. Not confessing true love. He licked his lips and forced his words through clenched teeth. "Sure. That'd be great."

He was definitely going to need more time.

Lori took a second piece of chocolate from Andy's bowl and unwrapped it with a frown. What was with Andy's suddenly pale face? He was probably overworking himself, spending too many hours at the office planning the retreat. It was one of the biggest events of the year for the teenagers, hence the reason she'd stopped by to see if he needed more volunteers. Summer had also offered to help, but she knew Andy would want to meet with her first. He always screened new workers.

Which was what she'd been trying to talk to him about when he suddenly resembled death on a plate.

She crinkled the silver foil in her hand. "I have another volunteer that could come, if you need the extra help."

"You should know with teenagers, the more help the better." The blood finally returned to Andy's face, and his smile looked a little more natural. Still, something shadowed his eyes. She really couldn't pry, though, not after she refused his offer to talk last Sunday. At least he hadn't stopped by the Chocolate Gator so far this week to check on her again. Was Bella having him spy? No, that was ridiculous. Bella called for updates herself every few days.

Though not since the freezer fiasco. Lori was dreading having that conversation, but she couldn't exactly skip it. It was amazing Andy hadn't found out yet, either.

"Who'd you have in mind to help?"

Lori jerked back to the present. "My coworker at your aunt's store. Summer Pierce."

"The Goth girl?" Andy's eyebrows shot up on his forehead.

"She's not Gothic. She just likes making statements." Lori threw the balled-up chocolate wrapper at him and grinned. "Something that should strike a chord with certain youth around here."

"Point taken." Andy tossed the foil back at her, and she ducked. It bounced off her purse and onto the floor. "Sure, bring her to church Sunday. I can meet her then. Or maybe I can swing by the shop tomorrow."

Lori shook her head so fast her head hurt. "No, I'll bring her Sunday." The last thing she needed was Andy coming by the store, waiting for her to mess something else up. At this rate, it was almost inevitable.

A wrinkle wove a fine line between his brows. "All right."

Lori stood and hiked her purse on her shoulder. She was being too obvious. It wasn't that she didn't want to be around Andy—she just didn't want him checking up on her as if she was a little kid. It was bad enough he'd never see her the way she always wanted him to. Poking around like a nosy big brother just poured salt on her existing wounds.

She said a quick goodbye and left the office before Andy could respond, her heart fluttering like a caged bird attempting escape. She was tired of being overlooked. Tired of being rejected. Tired of being the Friend and never the One.

Lori's heels clicked on the tile floor of the church, and she picked up speed before Andy could follow. It'd be best to focus her full attention on the shop for now. Forget about her secret admirer, whoever he was, and pour her energy into making the Chocolate Gator a success. Bella was the only person she needed to impress. The mystery gift-giver, if he was even real, was probably no different than any other guy. He'd get close and then hurt her, too. Just like Jason. Just like Andy.

Lori pushed through the doors of the church and headed for her car. She refused to look back toward Andy's office. From now on, she was only looking forward.

# Chapter Ten

It'd been a slow day so far at the Chocolate Gator. The few morning regulars hadn't shown up, and Lori refused to think about why or wonder if it was her fault. At least they'd recovered from her mistake with the freezer—though a ton of supplies weren't exactly necessary when there weren't any customers to purchase them.

Maybe she should chalk it up to the chilly February air and leave it that. In the meantime, she'd work on some ideas of how to get business booming again—and fast, before Bella returned and wondered where her livelihood had gone.

Lori's scrawled penmanship filled the paper with black ink.

1. *New window display.*
2. *Gimmick for sales—maybe a buy two, get one free offer? * Ask Bella first.*
3. *Offer gift wrap for holidays or special occasions.*

What else could she come up with? Lori tapped the pen against the counter. The customers that frequented the shop seemed relatively satisfied with her service and with the products they were buying. But there had to be something she was missing. "Summer, what makes a store interesting to you?"

"Black lights."

"I'm serious."

Summer looked up from the table she was wiping down and smirked. "So am I."

"Let me rephrase. What makes you want to visit a specific shop over and over?"

Summer's hand on the rag stilled. "Hmm. Good deals. Good customer service." She tilted her head to one side and grinned. "A cute salesclerk."

"We have all that."

"I've never seen a cute salesclerk around here."

"Thanks a lot. I meant the other stuff." Lori sighed and tapped harder with her pen. "I need something fresh."

The kitchen door opened, and Monny breezed through with a tray of chocolate cream puffs. "What about a sale?"

"I considered a buy two, get one free offer." Lori twisted on the stool to face Monny, proud of the way she didn't feel her cheeks burning. She could finally look him in the eye and not mentally kick herself for her blunder last week.

He set the cream puffs on the counter and dusted his hands on his apron. "Bella has made offers like that before. She puts a sign outside. It usually works well."

"Go for it." Summer resumed her cleaning.

"I should probably ask first."

"You're the temporary manager. It's your call, isn't it?" Monny paused by the kitchen door.

"I'm not sure." Lori worked her lower lip between her teeth. After the freezer incident, the day of lost profits and the baking disasters, she hated to assume anything.

"Come on, Lori. Be assertive." Summer tossed the damp rag across the counter to her.

Lori caught it and wound the rag between her fingers. Maybe

she should make a list. Pros—she could avoid bothering Bella while the woman was caring for her family. Plus, a few extra ingredients spent at the gain of more business would probably put them ahead profitwise.

Cons—it could seem presumptuous to make this kind of decision without Bella. But what was the worst that could happen?

"Let's do it!" Lori threw the rag back at Summer with a smile. "Monny, double your usual batch of chocolate croco-diles. We'll put the sign out this afternoon and run the sale for the rest of the week. We'll make it an early Valentine's special. Summer, find that board Bella uses to advertise, and some colored chalk. We'll make the advertisement now." She plucked a cream puff from the tray on the counter and held it up in a toast. "Here's to us!"

Lori took a big bite of the pastry as Monny and Summer hurried to follow orders. She might eat her words later, but for now, she'd focus on the cream puff.

Lori's dark brown hair glimmered with gold highlights in the sun as she crouched on the sidewalk, scrawling on a chalkboard in big, swirling letters. Andy slowed his pace, not wanting to interrupt her until she finished.

> *Valentine's Sale!*
> *Chocolate Crocodiles—Buy 2, Get 1 Free*
> *Limited Time Only!*

She stepped back from the board, clearly admiring the advertisement written in hot-pink chalk.

Andy stopped a few feet away, hands in his pockets. "I'll take a dozen."

Lori whirled to face him, revealing a brush of chalk on her cheekbone where she'd swiped her hair off her face. "Oh, really?"

"That'd be, let's see…six free chocolates?" He smiled.

"Doesn't work that way."

"Then you might want to add that to the fine print."

"I only have the big chalk sticks."

"Then it looks like you're out six pieces of chocolate."

Lori planted her hands on her hips, the chalk sticking out between her fingers. She was cute when frustrated, and probably didn't even realize she was marking on her jeans pocket as she stood there pouting. "Have you always been so stubborn?"

*Have you always been so adorable?* He just smiled, afraid to speak lest his thoughts jump out of his mouth.

"I guess I can make an exception for the boss's nephew." She stuck her tongue out at him.

"Mature. I think you've been hanging around the youth too much."

"Says the pastor who started a whipped-cream fight after the service." Lori grinned.

"Started *and* finished," Andy corrected. "Besides, that was months ago."

"Right, and you've grown up *so* much since then." Lori swiped at his arm with the chalk, dusting the fine hairs pink.

"Hey, I can start a chalk war just as easily." He reached for it, and she dodged out of his grasp, laughing, nearly tripping over the sign.

"You better not hurt my board!"

"It's fine." Andy straightened the sign to align with the shop window, then stepped back to view it fully. It would definitely catch attention with that hot-pink writing. "Why did Aunt Bella want to run a sale while she was gone?"

The teasing smile faded from Lori's lips. "She didn't. It was my idea."

"Are profits down?"

"A little." Her expression tightened, and so did Andy's

stomach. She was on to him, had to be. It explained her sudden distance and guarded response every time he asked about the store. What would he do now? He couldn't tell on his aunt and pass the blame. No, he'd just have to ease off a little, not check in so much. The shop would be fine—his friendship with Lori however, was growing questionable. Hopefully movie night this upcoming Friday would smooth the rough edges.

"I'm sure this sale will help. It's a good plan." Maybe a few compliments would bring the smile back to Lori's face. If not, then the gift that was waiting in his car for the opportune moment surely would.

She relaxed, her eyes thoughtfully studying his. "Thanks."

"Can you take a break for lunch?"

Lori opened her mouth, then paused. She looked over her shoulder at the store, then back to Andy. "Not really. I need to be around when this sale takes effect."

His heart dipped. "Right."

He wanted to hug her goodbye as usual, but knew better— not after such an obvious rejection. Did she really think a mob of chocolate consumers would be beating down the shop door in the next twenty minutes? Something was definitely up. Maybe she wanted to go to lunch with Monny instead.

Or maybe Lori had figured out the gifts were from him and didn't want them to be. She had been so withdrawn these last few weeks; the timing seemed too close to be coincidental. They used to go to lunch together all the time, back before he realized what Lori actually meant to him. Could she see the difference in his eyes?

Andy's head started to throb at all the *maybes*. He rubbed his hand through his hair in an attempt to shove back the frustration at Pastor Mike. If only the staff had left him alone about his love life, he'd still be happily ignorant of his heart's gravitation toward Lori. Naïveté was definitely underrated. Now he felt like a teenager with a crush. Except this wasn't a high-school fling. This was love. He swallowed hard. "I guess I'll see you tonight at the youth service, then."

"I might be late, but I'll come as quickly as I can." Lori's lips turned up in a smile that didn't quite register in her eyes. "See you there." She lifted her hand in a wave before slipping back inside the store.

Andy slowly shuffled toward his car parked in a lot a block away, kicking at a pile of dead leaves in his path. If Pastor Mike could see how hard this whole courting thing really was, maybe he'd get the church staff to ease off the pressure. He needed a break.

He unlocked his car door and sank onto the worn upholstery. The wrapped present on the passenger seat beside him caught his eye and felt like a punch in the abdomen. Part of him wanted to rush back into the Chocolate Gator with the gift and confess everything. But the louder, wiser part of him knew after Lori's behavior today, that would be the worst timing possible.

Andy tilted his head to rest against the back of the seat and closed his eyes, blocking the present from his view. He'd have to keep up the game awhile longer. Haley could deliver this one for him later this afternoon, and maybe after Lori saw the contents she'd be more open to him and his feelings.

There he went with the *maybes* again.

He started the car and eased out of the parking space, casting a long glance at the chocolate shop's window as he passed. Lori stepped onto the sidewalk, sliding sunglasses on her face and hiking her purse on her shoulder before taking off down the street.

Had to stick around for the sale, huh? Andy pressed his lips together and steered the car toward the church, his mind spinning almost as fast as the tires.

And *maybe* he was just a glutton for punishment.

Lori rubbed her finger over the gift card and frowned. A pair of trendy high heels marched across the front of the white plastic. It was hard to stay distant from her secret admirer when he just provided her with shopping money.

She had only been back from lunch for twenty minutes when an elderly woman brought the gift inside. The lady told Lori she was asked to deliver it anonymously, so her ruby-red lips were sealed. The twinkle in her eye hinted that was probably the most fun she'd seen in weeks, so Lori gave her a free crocodile for her trouble. The woman left happy, with chocolate crumbs stuck on her glossy lips, while Lori remained puzzled over the mysterious appearance of yet another present.

"This guy is good." Summer leaned against the counter on the opposite side from Lori and craned her head to see the gift card. "He must really know you well."

"It would seem that way." Which made it all the more frustrating not to know his identity. Lori tapped the card with her fingernail. "No signature, again."

"Not surprising. Don't worry, we'll figure out who it is sooner or later." Summer stretched, then paused, her arms still high in the air. "Wait a minute. What about that guy who you were talking to outside earlier?"

"Andy?" Lori snorted. "He's the youth pastor at my church."

Summer's arms lowered to her sides. "Why wouldn't it be him? It seems like he's always in the shop."

"We're just friends, and I help him with the youth group. He would never think of me that way." After years of hanging out and working together, that much was painfully obvious. Lori's eyes narrowed. "Besides, he's just here to check up on me for his aunt."

"He's Bella's nephew? Wow, small world." Summer adjusted one of the coils of spiked hair on her head and grinned. "He's cute, though."

Yes, he was. But that wasn't the point. Lori tucked the gift card in her purse under the counter. "I think we should get back to work."

"Right, because business is just booming." Summer rolled her eyes at the empty shop. "I think I hit a nerve, Boss."

"Keep going and you might." The last thing Lori needed to think about right now was Andy and the frustration that boiled over every time he poked around the store. Why couldn't he just come visit her because he wanted to see her? Because he missed her? He had to be spying for his aunt. Every time he showed up, he was asking about business. That was exactly the reason why she hadn't felt up to lunch with him earlier, and the reason she was already dreading movie night. She hated turning Andy down for lunch—especially since he usually paid—but today she wasn't up for defending the store or her methods of managing.

And she really didn't want Andy reporting back to Bella about that impromptu sale. After the freezer fiasco, Lori wondered how many more strikes she'd get. Hopefully the rules of baseball didn't apply to shop managing. At this rate, she'd blow through three strikes by next week.

Summer straightened from her slump against the counter, jerking Lori from her thoughts. "So, did you talk to Andy yet about my helping with the youth retreat?"

Lori nodded. "Yes, and he wants to speak with you about it on Sunday."

"Sounds good." Summer hesitated. "Are you sure your church won't mind—" she gestured toward her dark clothes and tattoos "—me?"

"You'll fit right in with the younger crowd."

"Right, because you're so ancient and all." Summer crinkled her nose at Lori.

"You know what I mean." Lori laughed. "Why don't you pick me up at nine o'clock?"

"Nine o'clock?" Summer moaned. "I always sleep until at least ten on Sundays. My church meets on Saturday nights."

"Exactly my point. If you're my ride, you have more motivation to get up." Lori reached under the counter and handed a crocodile to her. "Hush, and eat this."

"We're going to eat all our profits from the sale." Summer's protest didn't stop her from shoving the chocolate in her mouth.

Lori's gaze roved over the shop, taking in the sparkling clean floors, the perfectly arranged candy displays, the chairs tucked neatly under the shiny tables—and the obvious lack of patrons. She sighed. "What profits?"

## Chapter Eleven

"This is romantic-comedy night, isn't it?" Andy faked a groan as he collapsed against Lori's couch pillows. "I'd blocked it out." The truth was, he'd gladly sit with Lori and watch any movie she wanted. But he couldn't let her know that or they'd be drowning in chick flicks. Carter would never forgive him.

"That's right. Last month was action. The month before that was foreign. And November was drama." Lori popped a DVD into the player and grinned. "Get ready to cry."

"I don't cry at chick movies."

Lori quirked an eyebrow.

Andy cleared his throat. "That was *one* time. Even Carter teared up that night."

"Whatever." Lori's knowing grin made Andy's shoulders relax. Despite the awkwardness of the past few days, their friendship seemed to be back to normal—at least for tonight. He'd decided not to ask Lori about her lunchtime rejection from Wednesday. So far they'd avoided all talk about the Chocolate Gator, which seemed to be the reason for the unofficial truce. He'd take normal with Lori over awkward any day, even if he did have to be careful what he said—and watch a chick flick.

Andy moved a pillow aside as Lori sank onto the sofa, glad

she was sitting only one cushion away instead of across the room in the armchair. Probably because this was the best spot for seeing the TV, but a guy could hope, right?

"Whoops, forgot the popcorn." Lori started to stand, but Andy hopped up first.

"I'll get it." He grabbed the bowl from the counter, snagged a handful of napkins from the holder and set it on the coffee table in front of them. He sat back down, an inch closer than last time. Maybe if Lori forgot something else, he could eliminate that cushion distance between them once and for all. "Did you remember the chocolate?" He caught himself at Lori's look. "I know, I know, stupid question."

Lori reached for a pink bag on the end table. "Of course I remembered it. I brought a mixture from the store. And I still have some leftover Hershey's Kisses from my secret admirer."

Andy's heart stilled, then restarted with a heavy thud. "Still no clue who this mystery guy is?" He really hoped his voice sounded more natural to Lori than it did to his own ears. He cleared his throat.

Lori shrugged. "No, but I keep getting gifts." She grinned. "I figure at some point he'll get tired of spending money without credit for it."

"Probably." Andy thought of his thinning wallet. Good point. But he'd go into debt before confronting Lori with the truth too soon.

Lori aimed the remote at the DVD player and hit Play. "No crying, now."

Andy opened his mouth to argue, then shut it with a smile as Lori nestled against the cushions in her usual slumped position. They'd done movie nights with Carter and Gracie for coming on a year now, and each month it was always the same. Shoes off, legs tucked underneath her, head resting against the back of the couch. A few months ago, Lori had fallen asleep that way, and her head had drooped onto Andy's shoulder.

Maybe she'd be sleepy again tonight.

The opening credits rolled on the TV, and Andy tried to keep his mind on the movie. He should pay attention in case Lori wanted to discuss the film afterward. He adjusted his position on the couch and tugged a pillow into his lap, trying to get comfortable. On the screen, a bride sang a quirky love song, surrounded by her gushing attendants. His eyebrow twitched.

On second thought, it might be more productive to think about Lori, after all.

If Andy sat any closer, he'd be in the popcorn bowl. Lori swallowed, her dry throat having nothing to do with the salty snack. During the course of the movie, Andy had edged closer and closer until Lori wondered if it might be on purpose. But why would he do that? They'd never sat this close before—so close she could smell the fresh scent of laundry detergent on his shirt and feel the brush of fabric from his long sleeves as he reached for more popcorn.

Maybe she was just imagining his proximity because of her growing feelings. She'd never reacted this strongly to Andy's presence, but then again, usually movie night included Carter and Gracie. Between Carter and Andy's overly dramatic replaying of each scene, and Gracie's laughing protests, there had never been a chance for awkward tension.

The romantic comedy playing on the TV certainly didn't help Lori's raging emotions. If anything, it just made her want to cry. She could easily empathize with the redhead on the screen desperately trying to win her man, her best friend whom she'd never noticed until it was too late.

Unfortunately, Lori had seen this movie before, and she knew the ending.

She reached for another handful of popcorn at the same time Andy did, and their fingers brushed. An electric spark snapped, and Lori jerked, not sure if it was real or in her mind.

Beside her, Andy edged away a few inches, and she knew he felt it, too.

Felt it, and was putting distance between them.

She sipped from her can of soda, hoping to wash down the lump of disappointment in her throat. Whom she was kidding? Andy probably just realized how far he'd slumped over. He hadn't been close to her on purpose.

A few minutes later, the movie ended, bittersweet but leaving hope for the main character. Lori stood and pushed the stop button on the remote control, feeling sadder than she should after one of her favorite flicks. Unsure what to say to break the post-movie silence, she turned to pick up the popcorn bowl—just as Andy threw up his arms in a stretch. The bowl went flying and landed upside down on the floor, scattering bits of buttered kernels and husks on the carpet.

"My bad." Andy leaned down from the couch to grab it just as Lori squatted to do the same. Their heads collided with a thump, the collision knocking Andy off balance. He rolled off the couch and landed beside her.

"Are you okay?" they asked at the same time.

"I'm fine." Andy rubbed his forehead, then brushed his fingers against the sore spot on Lori's head. His featherlight touch sent shivers skating down her spine. "Are you?"

"Y-yes." She thought so, anyway. What was the question again? Staring into his eyes, Lori's frustrations about work and Andy's spy status melted away like hot fudge, and she forgot to breathe.

His touch gentled until he slowly slid his hand away from her face. They remained kneeling on the floor by the couch, side by side, eyes locked, not touching. But Lori felt his presence like a dozen close hugs. Was he going to kiss her? She leaned forward when Andy did, but after an achingly long moment, he sucked in his breath and stood.

Lori felt the rejection to her core, and she fumbled to stand.

Andy offered his hand to help, but the pain of tears pricking her eyes blended with the stabbing of her pride, and Lori struggled upright on her own.

Andy swallowed, his Adam's apple bobbing in his throat. He looked panicked, like he couldn't wait to leave. And why should he stay? The movie was over, and so was any chance of something developing between them. First the rejection of him moving away on the couch, then Lori's obvious misinterpretation of his actions. How stupid she must have looked, leaning in like that for nothing. Her chest burned under her sweatshirt, and she moved to eject the movie from the player before she embarrassed herself further.

"Uh, Lori, I…"

She widened her eyes to stop the tears threatening to pour and turned with a forced smile. "Want some chocolate to take home? I can grab a plastic baggie." She headed for the kitchen.

Andy stopped her with one arm, and she quickly turned in the other direction. "No, that's okay. Lori, seriously, I—"

"Wow, it's getting late. That was a long movie." Lori tapped her watch-free wrist, desperate to keep her voice natural. She couldn't let him know how he'd affected her, or she'd never be able to talk to him again. She couldn't lose their friendship, too. "I better get to bed. See you Sunday?" She ushered Andy toward the door, unsure how much longer she could keep the tears at bay.

Andy opened the front door, and a gust of cool night wind stung Lori's cheeks. She crossed her arms over her chest, around her heart, and waited, praying he'd leave without trying to explain his rejection.

"See you Sunday." Andy's heavy tone hinted that he wanted to say more, but Lori kept her eyes averted and that fake smile tight against her face.

"Have a good night."

Andy disappeared down the walk toward his car, and Lori

shut the door with a snap. Eyes closed, she slid against the door to a sitting position, resting her head against the hard wood. She shouldn't be surprised. Andy had never thought of her as anything more than a friend. But for that split second, kneeling beside him by the couch, surrounded by popcorn and pulsing hearts, her hopes had risen and whispered a possibility.

A possibility that continued to remain hopelessly, helplessly, impossible.

The organ music reached a closing crescendo, and Andy rose from the padded pew, tucking his Bible under his arm. Another Sunday come and gone, another lonely Sunday afternoon stretching long before him—and another Sunday of Lori not sitting with him at the service. Though after Friday night's awkwardness, he wasn't surprised Lori had chosen to sit elsewhere.

He couldn't believe he'd almost kissed her like that. How reckless could he be? Here he was trying to hide his identity as secret admirer, and he'd almost planted a big one on her at the first opportunity. She wasn't ready for the truth about his feelings yet, especially not after her panicked reaction to that near kiss. He apparently still had a lot of work to do to show her he was the man for her.

Andy turned to search the back rows of the church. Surely she was here somewhere. Wasn't she supposed to bring a friend to meet him about volunteering with the youth group? He almost hoped Lori hadn't made it, because then it wouldn't mean she was avoiding him—it would just mean she'd slept in or didn't feel good.

He treaded dejectedly behind the slow gait of the elderly gentleman heading down the aisle. He hoped to take Lori and her friend to lunch to discuss the retreat, but it looked like he would be eating alone again today.

"Andy! Andy, dear!" a voice warbled to his right. He turned to see Widow Spencer hobbling down the aisle toward him, pushing against the crowd like a salmon swimming upstream. Despite her frailty, she was making quick progress.

He was trapped.

Andy swallowed the automatic protest rising in his throat. Maybe she would say something other than how loud the youth service was every Wednesday. He braced himself for the attack as the widow moved to stand practically under his nose.

"You were alone again this morning. I take it you're still single?"

"Nothing changed since last week, ma'am." Andy forced his lips into a smile.

"Wonderful! Then you'll have no problem taking my great-granddaughter to dinner."

Not another one. First Pastor Mike, now the Widow Spencer. Apparently everyone in the church wanted him married off, ASAP. Andy mentally groaned but checked the sound before it could pop from his mouth. "I'm sure your great-granddaughter is lovely, Ms. Spencer. But I'm not really looking to date anyone right now."

He briefly closed his eyes, wishing he could afford to count to ten and ease away from his frustration before speaking. But that'd be too obvious to the woman. She'd been a member of the church forever—some said since the first service ever held—and was not someone he needed to offend.

He'd have to settle for squeezing his words out through clenched teeth instead.

"That's not what I hear from the pastor." Ms. Spencer's watery eyes shimmered behind her glasses, and she wagged a bony finger in Andy's face. "Eva is new to town. You two will really hit it off."

"But…"

"Then it's settled. Pick her up tomorrow night at six o'clock. Here's her address." She handed him a small sheet of paper.

"Ms. Spencer, I—"

"Don't be late. And wear green. It brings out your eyes." The elderly woman clutched her Bible to her chest and ambled away on her cane before Andy could speak another word.

*Great.* A blind date with Eva—whoever she was. What kind of woman required her grandmother to set her up on a date, and with barely a day's notice? Andy pinched the bridge of his nose between his fingers and blew out his breath. *One, two, three…*

"Andy, there you are!"

He opened his eyes in time to see Mr. Duvall, one of the deacons on staff, clap him on the shoulder. His firm grip lingered, and Andy awkwardly patted his back in return. "Good morning, Mr. Duvall."

"Excellent service, don't you think?"

"I agree."

"Especially the sermon." Mr. Duvall leaned forward, his eyes squinty with meaning. "Husbands loving their wives, wives honoring their husbands."

Andy gulped and hoped the older man didn't notice. "It was a good topic."

"Timely, eh?"

Andy's mouth opened, then shut. He was afraid to speak lest he lose it completely and run from the church with his arms thrown protectively over his head. He nodded instead.

"I thought so." Mr. Duvall laughed and slung his arm around Andy, shaking him slightly. "I thought so! I knew you had something up your sleeve."

"My sleeve? What?" Andy choked.

Mr. Duvall released his hold and stepped back. "No use denying it, son. I heard every word Widow Spencer said. I know you're going out with Eva tomorrow night. I knew you had your eye on someone!"

Someone whom he'd never actually seen before. Andy couldn't hold back the groan that burst from his lips. "Mr. Duvall, I really don't—"

"I was heading this way to ask about setting you up with my daughter."

Andy made a quick decision. One blind date was definitely more tolerable than two. "Right, well, too late, I suppose."

"Yes, too bad. But Eva's a nice girl. You kids have fun." Mr. Duvall winked before slipping back into the thick crowd still exiting the church building.

The parishioners heading toward the double doors and talking amongst themselves about lunch plans suddenly made him paranoid. How many more were plotting love matches for him? Who else had a granddaughter or niece that needed a date? Andy wanted to run as fast as the plush green carpet under his feet would allow but had the sinking feeling that would just draw more attention to himself. If he was about ten years younger, he'd slip belly-down under the pew like he did back when he was a kid, playing hide-and-seek with his Sunday school friends. Except this time he didn't want anyone to find him.

"Andy?" A familiar voice rang across the emptying auditorium, and he turned.

Okay, so maybe it was all right for *one* person to find him.

"Lori!" He hoped his smile seemed welcoming but not too excited. The fact that she sought him out after Friday night's incident said a lot. In fact, maybe—

"Andy, this is Summer."

Oh, yeah. Lori had a reason for finding him. Andy fought to hide his drooping smile as he extended his hand toward Summer, a short blonde who didn't look much older than his teenagers. "Nice to meet you." He shook Summer's hand. "I'm Bella's nephew."

"I know." Summer's edgy appearance slipped away with her bright smile. "I've seen you at the Chocolate Gator."

She *would* have to bring up the store. Andy glanced at Lori, but her face revealed nothing. If she was still angry about his pop-in visits, her expression didn't show it. Of course, after he'd nearly kissed her during movie night, Lori had more than just one reason to be angry with him. Andy tried to relax and keep his paranoia from his eyes as he turned his attention back to Summer. "So, how'd you like the service?"

"It was good. Different than my church, but I really liked it." She shrugged, and a teasing spark lit her eyes. "Lori said the youth services are more fun though."

His eyes darted back to Lori's face, and she blushed. "I didn't mean that in a bad way."

"I won't tell Pastor Mike, I promise." Andy grinned before turning back to Summer. "It'd be great if you wanted to check out our youth service next time. We meet on Wednesday nights. That way you could get to know the kids before the retreat."

"Sounds like a plan." Summer glanced back and forth between Lori and Andy, then checked her watch. "Oh, wow, I just remembered I promised I'd meet my parents for lunch. I better run. Andy, you can take Lori home, right? I'm going in the opposite direction." She began backing down the aisle.

Andy nodded, heart thumping at the implications of the sudden change in plans. "Sure—"

"Summer, wait!" Lori started after her, but the younger girl just waved and merged into the dissipating crowd moving toward the doors.

"What was that about?" Andy tried to laugh, but it sounded fake even to his own ears. He knew a matchmaking attempt when he saw one. Unfortunately, after Friday night, Summer's timing couldn't have been worse.

"I have no idea." Lori stared after Summer, and her eyes narrowed as if she might have a clue after all. "But I will definitely find out."

"I'm happy to take you home." Andy wasn't sure what Summer was up to, but he'd take it. "Want some lunch first?"

Lori let out a frustrated sigh. "I guess so."

Andy stacked Lori's Bible on top of his and then motioned toward the back doors. "I'm parked this way." It wasn't exactly a *yippee,* but, again, he'd take it.

## Chapter Twelve

"I saw the Widow Spencer corner you after church." Lori smirked before biting into a French fry. "Was she complaining about the noise in the gym on Wednesday nights again?"

"Thankfully, no." Andy leaned back against the hard plastic booth and shoved his empty wrapper away from him on the table.

"That's good." Lori swabbed another fry through her ketchup, trying to relax her tense shoulders. She'd definitely have to pay Summer back for this little matchmaking attempt of hers. So far, though, there'd been no talk about the disastrous movie night, and if Andy wasn't going to bring it up, she certainly wasn't going to, either. Maybe if they pretended nothing happened—rather, *almost* happened—their friendship could stay normal. "The widow is a sweet lady, but she goes on and on. Last time she caught me in the hall, I was late for the service."

Andy hesitated, then met her eyes across the table. "Actually, she was setting me up on a blind date with her great-grand-daughter."

Lori's half-eaten cheeseburger knotted in her stomach, and she paused, holding a fry near her mouth. "Really?"

"Apparently she thinks I'm perfect for Eva." Andy laughed, but it sounded forced. "I guess we'll see."

"You mean you're going?" The fry dropped to the table, and Lori desperately tried to discern the pounding of her heart—jealousy, pure and simple. It wasn't fair. Years of friendship left Andy completely oblivious to Lori, yet all it took was one meddling grandmother to make the perfect match for him and someone else.

She should have called her own granny years ago.

Andy took a sip of his drink. "I don't really have a choice."

Lori's head throbbed in her temples, and she shoved her food away, suddenly not nearly as hungry. "How can you not have a choice?"

"Are you mad?"

"Why would I be?" The answer sounded snippier than she meant it to, and she cleared her throat. "I mean, no." It's not like he had actually kissed her Friday night or shown any sign of feelings whatsoever. Andy was fair game.

To everyone but her.

Andy reached over and snatched a fry from her dismissed pile. "Then what's the problem?"

Lori drew a slow, steadying breath and forced herself to pick up her burger. Even if the idea of the date bothered her, she couldn't let Andy see that. Her mind raced with a suitable response. "I guess I'm just tired from working so much and this was surprising news."

"Take a day off. I'd be happy to fill in for an afternoon, if Summer couldn't cover for you." Andy swallowed a mouthful of fries. "Maybe you should go out with Monny."

"What? Why would I do that?" Lori reeled back in the booth. Had he seen through her jealousy and was now trying to push her toward another man? Since that near kiss, he was probably desperate to fend her off. Too bad she couldn't get a job in scaring men away. She'd be rich.

"I thought you had a thing for Monny, back when you thought the gifts were from him." Andy shrugged, but his eyes looked distant, like his mind was elsewhere. That, or there was something else he wasn't telling her.

Lori shook her head. "No, there's nothing. Monny and I are friends."

"Really?" Andy's voice squeaked and he cleared his throat. "I mean, you should take an afternoon off then anyway, have some alone time."

"No, that's okay. I can handle the store." Lori bit into the rest of her burger, but it tasted like sawdust. Sure, she could have alone time, while Andy and this Eva person mixed it up over dinner, laughed over candlelight. Her hand would brush his on the pristine tablecloth and—

"So, where are you two going?" Lori couldn't take it anymore. She had to know.

"Who?" Andy frowned.

"You and Eva."

"I don't know." Andy shrugged. "I'm surprised Widow Spencer didn't map out the entire evening for us right there in the church."

Was that discomfort on his face? Lori leaned closer in an attempt to discern Andy's features. Maybe he wasn't as excited about the matchmaking as she'd first thought. She edged farther toward the table, eyes narrowed in concentration.

"Careful, your hair is getting in your ketchup." Andy handed her a napkin and gestured toward her long brown hair now brushing against the messy wrapper.

*Great.* She dabbed at the red-tinged strands and forced a smile. "Thanks."

"What are friends for?" Andy winked before sliding out of the booth and picking up his paper cup. "Want a refill?"

Lori shook her head, watching as he wandered toward the soda dispenser near the front counter. She felt silly now that she had ever even considered Andy as her secret admirer. It was clear he never had—and never would—think of her in such a way.

She rested her head wearily against the back of the booth and closed her eyes. His parting words repeated in her mind, a numbing echo. *Friends.*

That's all she was ever destined to be with anyone.

"Need some help?"

Summer's voice penetrated Lori's concentration. With a start, Lori turned from the window display she was building. She'd been so involved in the chocolate construction and in reliving the details of yesterday's lunch with Andy that she hadn't even noticed it was time for Summer's shift. Funny, since earlier she'd been thinking of ways to torture Summer for her sudden departure from the church.

"Sure." Lori pursed her lips, not yet ready to give up her wild card. "Hand me the biggest of those red baskets over there."

She kept a sharp gaze on the younger girl as Summer handed over the basket. Who knew what other tricks Summer had up her sleeve? In a way, though, Summer had done Lori a favor. Her abandonment had paved the way for Lori to erase any lingering doubt about whether or not Andy could be her secret admirer. After hearing about his upcoming date with Eva, that last bit of hope had darted away faster than a crawfish from a net.

Lori tried to keep her expression casual as she took the basket and stretched to place it next to the glass pane. "How was school?"

"Fine—for a Monday, anyway." Summer shuffled her feet on the tile floor.

Silence filled the space around them.

Summer cleared her throat. "How's business today?"

"Decent." Lori stepped off the window's platform and picked up the heart-shaped confetti she'd found on sale over the weekend. "I hope this new display will bring in some window-shoppers." She sprinkled it over the floor of the display.

Summer fiddled with a plastic bag of shiny red cut-out lips. "I'm sure it will."

Lori stepped back to admire her progress. "I'm actually considering taking your advice and applying for a loan for my own shop soon. It never hurts to try, right?"

"Really? That's great." Summer smiled, then her eyes turned wary.

Lori kept working—and waiting.

Suddenly, the bag dropped to the floor at Summer's feet, and she blew out her breath in a huff. "Okay, okay, let me have it. I know you're just dying to get me back for leaving you yesterday."

"Last time I checked, Cupid didn't need a helper." Lori crossed her arms over her chest and tried to keep her frown. But Summer's nervous expression just made her want to laugh.

Summer picked up the bag of lips and tossed it on the window platform. "I know, and I'm sorry. I saw an opportunity and took it. I just really think you and Andy—"

"It doesn't matter what you think." Lori ripped open the plastic bag, her frown suddenly feeling much more natural. "Andy's a friend. That's all he wants to be. Okay?"

Summer passed her a stuffed teddy bear. "If you say so."

"I do." Lori set the teddy bear in the big red basket and forced a smile. "It's not meant to be, all right? And that's how I want it."

The lie burned her lips, but Lori kept from offering further explanation as they worked on the display. Summer didn't understand. She thought she'd been trying to help, and maybe in a way she had. If Andy was going to be dating this Eva person, then maybe Lori could finally shove him out of her thoughts for good. She could keep being Andy's friend, and hopefully he'd never know the difference, never know she'd fallen for him.

Maybe Andy's constant obliviousness could be a good thing, for once.

Lori crawled into the window to spread another layer of confetti over the platform. Her back pressed against the cool glass, and she scooted the basket with the bear farther to the left.

"Ready for the candy?" Summer held up a brick of chocolate wrapped in the Chocolate Gator's signature foil.

Lori gazed around the side of a giant stuffed alligator, wearing a red bow. "Yes, and that roll of ribbon." She caught the spool Summer tossed and used scissors to create festive curls. Then she tied the pink ringlets to the handle of the basket, now stuffed with fluffy cotton. The chocolate brick sat in front, nestled amidst the loose confetti. The Valentine's display was almost complete, but Lori still didn't like where the stuffed gator was positioned. He should be front and center, as was the name of the shop.

She frowned. "Summer, would you go outside and see what you think from the sidewalk? Something needs to be changed, but I don't know what. It's just not working."

"Sure." Summer pushed open the door and stepped outside. Lori scooted to the far end of the platform so Summer could view the arrangement, but the high heel of Lori's shoe caught in the weave of the basket.

Summer tapped the glass, and Lori craned her head to see behind her, one leg stuck awkwardly to the side. "Hold on!" She pulled on her shoe, but it didn't budge.

This was great. Hopefully the sidewalks full of shoppers would remain oblivious to her predicament until Lori freed herself. The store needed attention, granted, but not the live-action kind. She tugged harder.

A loud but muffled voice snagged her attention, and Lori peered over her shoulder again to see Summer taking a wrapped gift from the same little old lady who had delivered the last one.

Her hopes lifted, and she momentarily forgot about her shoe. Lori beat on the glass. "Summer!"

Summer waved her off and kept talking, but her voice wasn't audible through the window. Lori pressed her face close to the window, eager to catch a few words. Maybe Summer was asking the woman who had given her the present to pass on information about its sender. Would today be the day Lori's mystery man was finally revealed? Her heart pounded.

And her ankle hurt. Lori groaned at her trapped foot and turned so her leg wasn't twisted at such an angle. What was Summer saying? She peered back over her shoulder and ignored the cramp in her neck.

Summer had balanced the blue-and-brown polka-dotted box on her hip and was gesturing wildly with her free arm. The elderly lady backed away, shaking her head, her bright red lips pursed. Summer stepped forward, still talking, but the woman turned and started down the sidewalk, purse banging against her side at her fast clip.

There went their only lead. Had Summer lost it completely? Lori wanted to know who her admirer was, too, but she wasn't about to pester old ladies to get the answer. She slipped her foot out of her shoe and grabbed it with both hands, yanking with all her strength. She never thought there would be a day where she actually regretted not wearing sneakers, but today was pretty close.

• The heel popped free of the basket, and Lori fell against the window with a thud. She straightened just in time to see Andy and a horde of tourists laughing at her through the other side of the glass.

Andy took the chair opposite Lori, while Summer perched on the edge of a nearby table. He'd stopped by the shop to check on things and saw Lori sprawled in the front window, a curious crowd gathered to watch, and Summer arguing with an elderly woman. Good thing Aunt Bella wasn't here, or she'd have flipped.

Actually, she probably would have offered the crowd a sale on chocolate and secured a whole new batch of customers. He mentally beat his head on the table for not thinking of it before he shooed the onlookers away.

Lori rubbed her ankle with both hands. "That window display better be worth it." She held her foot out for inspection. "No bruising."

"Yet." Summer snorted. "Next time, maybe we should hire someone to do the display."

"If you'd been helping me instead of harassing the elderly, I wouldn't have gotten stuck." Lori tried to frown, but a laugh poked through the attempt. "I guess we did look pretty silly."

"That's an understatement." Andy rested his arms on the tabletop. "The window part I get. But is anyone going to explain to me why Summer was bothering an old lady?" He paused. "Now, there's a question I never thought I'd ask."

"I wasn't trying to bother her," Summer huffed. "I was trying to ask who gave her that gift to deliver."

Andy's heart skipped a beat, then thudded with a start against his chest. "What gift?" But he had the distinct feeling he already knew exactly which one.

"That one." Lori gestured to the front counter, where Andy noticed for the first time the polka-dotted package sitting by the register—the same package Andy had sent Haley to deliver an hour ago.

He tried to keep his expression neutral. "Who is that for?" *Stupid, stupid, stupid.* His secret-admirer game had almost gotten him busted and Summer in trouble. Haley must have not found an opportunity to sneak the gift inside without being seen and had gone for backup in the form of blue hair and glasses.

"It's for me." Lori raised her hand.

"Another secret-admirer present?"

"Apparently." Lori hopped up—on her supposedly injured ankle—and snagged the box from the counter. She hugged the present to her chest. "This same lady has delivered two gifts now, and while I was trapped in the window, Summer was trying to get her to reveal who sent it."

Summer shifted positions on the tabletop. "I think I got on

# Get 2 Books FREE!

## Love Inspired Books,
### publisher of inspirational fiction,
## presents

**A series of contemporary love stories that will lift your spirits and reinforce important lessons about life, faith and love!**

**FREE BOOKS!**    Use the reply card inside to get two free books by outstanding inspirational authors!

**FREE GIFTS!**    You'll also get two exciting surprise gifts, absolutely free!

# GET 2 BOOKS

**IF YOU ENJOY A ROMANTIC STORY** that reflects solid, traditional values, then you'll like *Love Inspired®* novels. These are heartwarming inspirational romances that explore timeless themes of forgiveness and redemption, sacrifice and spiritual fulfillment.

We'd like to send you two *Love Inspired* novels absolutely free. Accepting them puts you under no obligation to purchase any more books.

## HOW TO GET YOUR
## 2 FREE BOOKS AND TWO FREE GIFTS

1. Return the reply card today, and we'll send you two *Love Inspired* novels, absolutely free! We'll even pay the postage!

2. Accepting free books places you under no obligation to buy anything, ever. The two books have combined cover prices of at least $11.00 in the U.S. and at least $13.00 in Canada, but they're yours to keep, free!

3. We hope that after receiving your free books you'll want to remain a subscriber, but the choice is yours—to continue or cancel, any time at all!

## EXTRA BONUS

You'll also get two free mystery gifts! (worth about $10)

# FREE!

**BUSINESS REPLY MAIL**
FIRST-CLASS MAIL    PERMIT NO. 717    BUFFALO, NY

POSTAGE WILL BE PAID BY ADDRESSEE

THE READER SERVICE
PO BOX 1867
BUFFALO NY 14240-9952

NO POSTAGE
NECESSARY
IF MAILED
IN THE
UNITED STATES

the lady's nerves with my questions, but she seemed nervous before I even started talking to her. I thought she was going to hit me with her purse."

"You can come across as a little intimidating." Lori flicked the sleeve of Summer's black top, revealing another tattoo.

"So I hear." Summer rolled her eyes.

Andy cleared his throat. "Well, if everything is okay here, I guess I better get going." He didn't want to leave, but he wasn't sure he could hide his reaction when Lori opened that present. This gift was a little more personal, a little more revealing, and he couldn't afford to ruin everything now by slipping up in front of Lori. She wasn't ready for the truth yet, not while their friendship was still so sketchy—and especially not after the last movie night. At least now he knew she wasn't interested in Monny. One less obstacle in his path.

Only three hundred or so to go. If only he could be certain she was ready to date again after Jason. But asking without seeming obvious would be tricky.

"Why'd you stop by, anyway?" Summer brushed her bangs out of her eyes, now lit with a curious gleam. "You just showed up out of nowhere."

"I was in the area." He darted a nervous glance at Lori, who was examining the box, probably searching for a name tag. *Good luck.*

"And you thought you'd stop by?" Summer smirked. "That's how it goes, right?"

She was teasing him. Normally he'd tease right back, but Lori was already tugging the bow free on the wrapping, and he had to get away before she saw the leather Bible cover with her name engraved on the front.

"Something like that." Andy stood so fast he nearly tripped over the chair leg. He caught his balance and continued to backpedal. "I'll see you girls later."

Summer waved, but Lori only grunted, immersed in removing the layers of tissue paper from the box. Andy turned and made steady progress toward the door, forcing himself not to look back. He'd go to his office and get some work done before his dreaded date with Eva. Maybe he could make it through the evening if he kept his mind on the future—a future that hopefully involved Lori at his side.

The sound of a box lid hitting the ground and Lori's excited gasp drifted in his wake as Andy strolled onto the sidewalk, and he couldn't help the smile that turned up his lips as he continued to his car.

# Chapter Thirteen

Utensils clanked on plates, kitchen doors bustled open and shut, and fellow diners hummed with various conversations from their tables. But the busy background noise of the restaurant couldn't come close to covering Eva's piercing, high-pitched laugh.

Andy's eyes narrowed as the pulse in his temples increased. It was amazing the decibel this woman could reach when giggling. If his ears didn't ache so badly, he'd imagine only dogs could hear it.

"I'm so glad we came," Eva gushed. She reached for a roll on the table between them and set it on her plate, flipping her long, curly blond hair over her shoulder for what had to be the fiftieth time. "You're so funny."

He wasn't—actually, Andy had been trying his hardest to be completely, one hundred percent boring so as not to invoke that awful screech. No wonder the girl needed her great-grandmother to set her up on dates. She was attractive—until she opened her mouth and made all of the earth's creatures run for their lives.

Andy sipped from his glass of iced tea and wondered how he could subtly flag the waiter for their check. It wasn't just the laugh that had him gritting his teeth, nor was it the constant hair flipping, the ditzy speech and the fact that she had ordered the most expensive steak on the menu. Those weren't her worst qualities; in fact, she had only one unforgivable characteristic.

She wasn't Lori.

Widow Spencer was going to be crushed, and Eva was going to be dateless come next weekend. But Andy couldn't pretend any longer. It wasn't fair to him or the woman—or his ears.

The waiter appeared at their table with refills for their drinks, and Andy caught his eye and nodded. In a flash, he was back with their check, and Andy reached for his wallet so fast his finger snagged in his back pocket.

"So, what's next?" Eva shoved her half-full plate away from her, and Andy winced. Might as well be a rolled-up twenty lying there next to the scoop of untouched mashed potatoes. Strange, since he had no problem dropping three times that on Lori's gifts.

"Next?" Andy hesitated, tapping his fork against his plate. *Next* he wanted to take Eva home as fast as the speed limit would allow and collapse on his couch, alone, with nothing but his favorite pajama pants and the TV remote control for company.

"Want to go dancing?" Eva shimmied in her seat, Andy supposed as an example of her dancing ability. "Or catch a late movie?"

"I don't really dance." It was true, he didn't. Not with blind dates, anyway.

"Then what about ice cream? Or coffee?"

"I'm really full."

Eva's face darkened. "I see."

A sudden burst of sympathy overrode the lingering annoyance, and Andy reached against the table toward her. Just because he couldn't get past his thoughts for Lori didn't mean he had to be rude. "Listen, Eva, it's not personal. I'm just not really in a good position to date right now."

"Then why'd you take me out?"

Andy opened his mouth, then shut it, not wanting to rat out Ms. Spencer.

Understanding dawned in Eva's expression, and her lips pursed. "It was my great-grandmother, wasn't it? She made it sound like you asked about me, but I bet she forced you into this." Her grip tightened on Andy's wrist. "She's so meddling."

Andy tugged at his hand, to no avail. "Eva, I'm really sorry. I didn't mean for—"

"Well, it looks like you two are hitting it off." Lori suddenly appeared at the table's edge, Summer standing a few steps to her right.

"Lori!" Andy wrenched his hand free and rubbed it with his other one. "What are you doing here?"

She tossed her hair over her shoulder, yet somehow the movement wasn't nearly as aggravating as when Eva did it. "Summer was on a vegetarian kick last month and had a meat craving tonight. They have the best burgers here."

"Yeah, turns out I'm a beef girl after all." Summer's gaze drifted to Eva's half-empty plate. "Hey, are you going to finish that?"

Eva blinked twice. "No, I'm done."

"Summer!" Lori nudged the younger girl in the ribs and rolled her eyes. "We better go order before she starts snatching food." She smiled, but it looked somewhat forced as Lori's eyes darted between Andy and Eva.

A knot welled in Andy's throat. "Lori, I'm not… It's not…" His pathetic attempt at an explanation died on his lips as the girls continued following the hostess to a table across the floor.

Eva's gaze locked on Andy, and she folded her arms across her chest. "Not really dating right now, huh?"

"Trust me, Lori and I aren't dating." He rubbed his temples with his fingers.

"But you want to."

"It doesn't really matter." Or maybe it did. That look on Lori's face couldn't have been jealousy, could it? He replayed her expression in his mind as he stared absently at his glass of tea. There had definitely been a tight smile and a twitching eyebrow involved. Apparently his date with Eva had bothered Lori more than she wanted to admit.

Maybe it was time to rethink the timing of his secret-admirer revelation. After all, they'd had a great time at lunch together yesterday, and she hadn't tried to bite his head off when he showed up at the store. That was significant. Maybe he should just put it all on the line and share his heart with her.

Eva snorted, drawing Andy's attention back across the patterned tablecloth. "Of course it matters to you. I might wear contacts, but I can see what's right in front of me." She sighed and mumbled under her breath, "It's always the cute ones."

Andy couldn't help but glance across the restaurant to Lori's table. She sat facing in his direction, the menu partly covering her face, but there was no mistaking the way her eyes flicked to his and then back down at the laminated plastic. Hope tingled up his spine.

Eva coughed. "Can you at least give me the dignity of taking me home before you start mooning over another woman?"

"Sure." He stood and pulled out her chair for her, then helped her into her jacket. It wasn't Eva's fault he was in love with someone else. Probably wasn't entirely her fault her laugh could shatter a window, either.

"After you." He guided Eva toward the front door, mind already drifting to Lori's table near the kitchen. She'd probably order a salad, then a big chocolate dessert to make up the difference.

And hopefully talk about him between forkfuls.

Lori dropped her fork on her plate, too upset to finish her dessert. She squinted at the towering chocolate volcano and sighed. Whom was she kidding? She grabbed her fork again and stabbed it into the melting mass of ice cream. The nerve of Andy, flaunting his date and being all gentlemanly. A regular Romeo. And what did she get? Burgers and fries on a Sunday afternoon—dutch treat.

Why didn't Andy think of her as dating material? *Stab.* Eva was pretty, but she wasn't a supermodel. *Stab.* What did she have that Lori didn't? *Stab, stab.* And why did it take a nosy grandmother to fix him up when Lori had been around and available for years?

A blob of ice cream slipped out of the dish and slid toward Summer. She covered her plate with her hand in defense. "Hey, what'd that ice cream ever do to you?"

"Sorry." Lori scooted the rest of her dessert toward the center of the bowl. "I'm just frustrated."

"Don't worry. Andy wasn't into her." Summer forked a piece of steak into her mouth.

"That's not what…" Lori paused. "How can you tell?"

"He looked miserable until he saw us. Like we had rescued him or something."

Lori shook her head. "I've told you before that Andy's not interested in me." She glanced over at the empty table Andy and Eva had vacated. "Trust me, we're just friends. He's made that abundantly clear." Way, *way* too many times.

"Whatever. I still think there's a chance Andy is your secret admirer." Summer held the ketchup bottle over her plate and pounded on the bottom.

"It wouldn't make sense. We've been friends for years, so why now? Besides, he's such a prankster." Lori traced a design in her chocolate with her fork. "These gifts have had a romantic edge to them. It's just not Andy. He'd send someone a whoopee cushion before he'd send sweet, personalized gift cards." She smirked. "The only flowers he'd send would squirt water." All part of his charm. Romance was nice, but laughing together was even more fun. Jason had been stodgy, technical, never given to food fights or fun. Andy was perfect for Lori.

Too bad he was also blind.

Summer leaned back to make room for the waiter refilling her glass of water. "I guess. You know Andy better than I do."

Lori nodded slowly, but her heart argued. She used to know him. Lately she and Andy had drifted apart, and it started the day she began work at the Chocolate Gator. It was probably her fault. Every time he showed up at the shop, she grew so defensive. But why did he have to check on her all the time? She didn't enjoy feeling like a failure, especially in front of him.

Lori set her fork on her plate with a clatter. "You want any of this?"

Summer's eyes bugged. "Lori not finishing her chocolate?" She shook her head. "You really do have it bad."

"I do not." The words felt like a lie. Lori sipped from her glass of water as she tried to decipher her feelings. She did have a thing for Andy, and it seemed like the more she fought it, the bigger it grew. A year ago, Lori would have admitted to admiring Andy, maybe even having a crush on him. But it had never gone further than that in her mind because she knew their friendship was an important part of both their lives and didn't think it was worth risking.

When had that changed? Lori traced a path in the condensation on her glass. At some point, without her noticing, those feelings of admiration and friendship had morphed into jealousy and the intense need for Andy to see her as a competent and successful woman, not just a girl to play ball with or help at the church.

"Earth to Lori! Come in, Boss!" Summer nudged her leg under the table. "If you don't have it bad, then where'd you go just now?"

"Just thinking."

"About Andy." Summer shot her a knowing look.

"Whatever." Lori shook her head, determined to clear it of all these crazy misconceptions. Her feelings for Andy might have changed, but there was no reason why she couldn't deny them until they went away. Letting them develop further was completely pointless. His sitting at a table with Eva moments ago only further proved her point.

Summer patted her stomach. "That was really good. Remind me of this meal next time I get a random vegetarian urge."

"Will do." Lori gestured to the waiter that they were ready for their check. She wanted to get out of there and go home before her traitorous mind could imagine what Andy and Eva would do next. Maybe take a moonlit walk around the city, or enjoy a ride on the trolley. Or share beignets at Café Du Monde.

Lori's lips pressed together. They'd probably even sit at the same table she and Andy always shared, in the back corner— far enough away from the kitchen to be out of the hectic bustle, but close enough to smell the fried bread.

The waiter brought their bill, and Lori quickly slipped a wad of cash onto the check holder, almost forgetting to count it first. Despite the jealousy knotting her stomach, it really didn't matter whether Andy and Eva became a couple or not—because Lori and Andy never would. The sooner she could discover the identity of her secret admirer, the sooner she could rid herself of these nagging feelings for Andy and move on with Mr. Right.

Whomever he was.

## Chapter Fourteen

Andy tossed a runaway basketball back across the gym floor to one of their youngest youth-group members. "Try to keep it in the court, man. We've got ladies here who don't particularly like getting hit in the head."

The boy caught the ball and grinned at the flock of junior-high girls frantically fixing their hair from the near hit. "Sure thing, Pastor."

Andy shook his head as he stacked another couple of folding chairs. Usually the guys helped him clean up the gym after the Wednesday-night services, but tonight they seemed distracted. Summer had visited the church again with Lori, which was probably the reason. The kids thought it was cool that Summer looked like them.

He glanced at Lori as he worked, wondering if she was upset about his date with Eva Monday night or if those signs of jealousy had existed only in his imagination. It'd been torture staying away from the Chocolate Gator yesterday, but showing up uninvited again would probably hurt rather than help his fledgling romance with Lori.

Andy's cell phone rang from his jacket pocket, and he fished it out. "Hello?" He shouldered the cell while stacking another group of chairs.

"Andy, my man. What's happening?" Carter's cheerful voice boomed.

"Not much, honeymooner. Just cleaning up from the youth service." Andy winced at the metal clanking as one chair hit another harder than he'd intended.

"This is one honeymoon that's over. We're on our way home."

"Back to the real world, huh?"

"Unfortunately." Carter paused. "But I suspect the real world will be much more interesting now."

Andy laughed. "I'm sure Gracie is eager to get back to those penguins of hers at the aquarium, too." Gracie was a penguin keeper at the Aquarium of the Americas.

"No doubt." Carter cleared his throat. "Listen, man, I was just calling to check on the whole situation with Lori. Have you told her how you feel yet, or are you still playing the secret-admirer role?"

"I haven't been able to tell her yet." Andy glanced over his shoulder to make sure no one could overhear his conversation. "But in the meantime, everyone at the church who even knows someone single is trying to set me up on dates."

"Bummer."

"You have no idea." Andy gave a quick recap of his date with Eva. "And to make matters worse, Lori showed up at the same restaurant and saw me."

"Ouch."

"No kidding."

Carter clicked his tongue. "Maybe you should come clean."

"Not after the disaster with Eva."

"I don't know what to say, man. You'll have to tell her the truth eventually, and I really believe the sooner the better in this case."

"I'm not as sure." Andy loaded the last of the folding chairs onto the rolling cart and began to push it toward the storage closet. "I just wish I could know she felt the same way about me."

"Love is a risk, dude. You know that."

"I do. And Lori's definitely worth the risk. I just don't know if I'm ready to handle her rejection. Our friendship means too much to me to risk losing it if she isn't interested."

"Maybe she'll surprise you."

Maybe. Or maybe she'd break his heart into ten thousand tiny pieces and scatter them across St. Charles Avenue. Andy briefly closed his eyes. "I appreciate the positive thought."

"No problem. Hang in there, and keep us posted. We'll get together as soon as the missus and I get settled into our new house."

"Sounds good." Andy said goodbye and dropped his cell back in his pocket, then bent to shove the chair cart into the closet.

"Pastor Andy?"

He jumped. The cart, still rolling with momentum, slammed into the back shelf of the storage room. A dozen basketballs and foam bats rolled onto the floor.

"My bad." Haley scooted past him into the closet and bent to pick up the sports equipment.

"How long were you standing behind me?" Andy narrowed his eyes, hoping Haley hadn't overheard his conversation with Carter. She already knew about his feelings for Lori, but he didn't want to broadcast his bad date with Eva.

"Not long." Haley shoved a ball back onto the shelf, then met his waiting gaze. "Okay, fine, long enough. I heard you had a bad date."

"Haley—"

"I won't tell anyone, I promise." Haley held up both hands in the Scouts-honor position. "But that reminds me. I know a girl who'd be perfect for you, and I really think—"

"No." Andy tried to keep his voice even, though every frustrated instinct inside him wanted to slam the door and lock Haley in the closet. "Not a chance."

"But just listen—"

"No more blind dates."

"This girl is different."

"Aren't they all?" He rubbed his palms down the length of his face and groaned. This wasn't happening. When had his love life degenerated to blind dates set up by elderly parishioners and meddling teenagers?

"Trust me." Haley pleaded with her eyes, her hands practically wringing a foam bat. "You won't be sorry."

He was already sorry. Andy exhaled loudly, knowing he should count to ten—make that one hundred—before he said anything in anger.

Haley must have taken his silence for interest. "Seriously, she's great. A friend of a friend—and she's your age, so don't worry about that."

Age was the least of his concerns right now, though he supposed it was the main concern of the senior pastor and the rest of the church staff. Andy pressed his lips together. If that one sorry excuse for a youth minister at that church across town hadn't made such a poor decision, Andy wouldn't even be in this mess right now. He should call him up and—

"Pastor Andy?"

He jerked back to reality, where Haley still waited for a response. "Listen, Haley, I appreciate the thought, but I'm not interested."

"It's because of Lori, isn't it?"

He looked over his shoulder with panic, holding one finger to his lips. The teens remaining in the gym were still gathered around Lori and Summer, talking animatedly amongst themselves. Lori tilted her head back and laughed, her long brown hair falling across her back.

Andy clenched a kickball between both hands. He would

prefer getting slammed by one of those foam bats Haley held than deal with the constant, gnawing ache in his stomach every time he saw Lori.

"Your secret is safe with me," Haley piped up.

Andy raised one eyebrow. "And Jeremy."

Haley twirled one braid around her finger and winced. "Right. But I tell him everything."

"I hope he doesn't feel that way about someone else."

"We won't tell anyone, I promise. Lori will figure out the gifts soon enough, anyway. Do you have another one for me to deliver?"

"I think I'm mailing them from now on." Since the disaster with Summer, the old lady and Lori's window display, it seemed best to keep it simple, even if it meant his packages took longer to arrive.

"Okay." Haley crossed her arms and tapped her foot, obviously still waiting.

Andy crossed his arms right back. "I'm not giving on this one. No more blind dates."

She cocked one hip to the side in her traditional stubborn pose. "Would you just think about it?"

Andy opened his mouth to refuse, then stopped. Pastor Mike was leaning against the counter in the kitchen area of the gym, talking to a few of the parents. One woman looked agitated and gestured wildly with one arm—in Andy's direction? Andy swallowed hard. The man beside her kept pounding one fist in his hand, and nodding toward his daughter, who stood talking to Lori and Summer.

Was this about him? Paranoia crept over Andy's shoulders and settled like a dark blanket. What if Lori never accepted him as anything more than a friend? Would he really lose his job if he didn't get serious about a woman soon? Surely the senior staff wouldn't be that harsh.

But the stern expression on Pastor Mike's face caused a

finger of doubt to trail down Andy's spine. He shifted his weight and glanced back at Haley's hopeful face. He was running out of options, and fast. What was the worst that could happen? He tried to shove aside the memory of Eva's laugh and drew a steadying breath.

"Set it up."

Lori couldn't help but smile as she watched Summer talk with the youth-group members that stuck around after the service. They were hitting it off great. At this rate, the retreat would be a success, and Andy could have that much more pressure taken off him from being understaffed.

"Lori!"

Lori turned from the conversation in time to see Haley maneuvering through the gymnasium, eyes bright and cheeks flushed. "Hey, there. You look excited."

"I had a super idea." Haley tugged Lori's arm, pulling her slightly away from Summer and the other teens.

Lori ducked her head toward Haley. "Let's hear it."

"I know the perfect guy for you."

Lori let out her breath in a slow rush and checked to make sure no one had overheard. Perfect guys didn't exist. But no use bursting Haley's bubble at this young age. "Who would that be?"

"It's a friend of a friend." Haley beamed. "He's meeting you for lunch Friday at Café Du Monde."

"What? Haley, no." Lori's thoughts raced together in a tangled maze. She couldn't meet a stranger for lunch, supposedly perfect or not. "I can't."

"What about Saturday, then?"

"No, I mean I can't date a complete stranger. Ever."

"Come on, he's a great guy. You'll have a blast." Haley nudged her arm and winked. "He's cute, too."

"Well, in that case…" Lori rolled her eyes. *"No."* The steady thump of a basketball across the gymnasium echoed her pound-

ing heart. Did she seem so desperate for love that she'd resort
to a blind date set up by a member of the youth group? How
embarrassing. But Haley couldn't have known about Monny,
or her feelings for Andy, or even about Jason and their past. So
why the setup?

"Please, Lori, it's already planned. He'd be really disappointed if you didn't show." Haley clutched her hands together.
"Just one date. Not even a date, really—just lunch."

Lori shook her head.

"Seriously. One beignet, then you can leave if you don't like
him."

Lori nibbled on her bottom lip. It didn't sound *that* bad when
Haley put it that way—unless this mystery man had the same
plan and ended up ditching Lori before she could ditch him. She
frowned. She was definitely not up for any more rejection, especially from a complete stranger—and especially not with
Valentine's Day breathing down her neck. The holiday would
be difficult enough to go through alone, without an extra memory
of embarrassment lingering. She had plenty of those already.

Haley held her breath, waiting, bouncing on the soles of her
shoes. Lori stopped the *no* hovering on her lips and paused.
Haley seemed excited—really excited. What if she knew something Lori didn't? What if her secret admirer was someone at
the church and had put Haley up to this as a means of revealing his identity? She could be blowing her chance by refusing.
Better yet, if it was her secret admirer, then she obviously
wouldn't be rejected first, but would have the option of doing
the rejecting.

"I'll do it." Lori covered her ears at Haley's squeal. "Just
this once!"

"You'll have fun, I promise. This guy is so perfect for you."
She gave Lori an excited hug.

"Whatever you say." Lori hugged her back, then held Haley
at arm's length, gripping her shoulders and lowering her head

to Haley's level so she could see the girl's eyes. "No more making plans without asking me first, okay?"

"Deal."

Lori released her grip, and Haley scooted across the gym toward Jeremy. Summer caught Lori's gaze and raised her eyebrows. "Later," Lori mouthed. She rejoined the conversation, but her head wasn't in it. She was already nestled at a corner table at Café Du Monde with her mystery man.

Problem was, in her fantasy, her mystery man had Andy's face.

# Chapter Fifteen

The rich aroma of warm beignets and powdered sugar filled the air as Lori stood in line at Café Du Monde. She rubbed shaky hands down the front of her jeans. How could she have agreed to a blind date with a total stranger? The odds of it being her secret admirer were pretty slim. She must have gotten caught up in Haley's excitement and lost all sense of logic. She hadn't done something this silly since dropping a hundred dollars on a pair of polka-dot shoes.

The man in front of her stepped closer to the counter, and Lori inched behind him, keeping her head lowered. She peered from beneath her curtain of hair at the crowded restaurant, searching the maze of tables for a man sitting alone. So far, no one fit the description Haley had offered. Blond hair, average build, late twenties. Great smile.

Lori took another step forward. What if she got stood up? She'd be mortified. Haley wasn't exactly the best secret-keeper in the church. If that happened, the entire congregation would soon be offering their stream of condolences and matchmaking schemes. She'd forever be the girl getting set up with someone's great-nephew or grandson or third-cousin-twice-removed.

She'd rather take a vow of celibacy.

A flash of blond hair at a far table caught Lori's eye, and her heart launched in her chest like a rocket at takeoff. Was it him?

Lori scooted around the man in front of her for a better view, but the blond's back was to her—a very nice, muscular back. She clutched the strap of her favorite flowered purse. She could do this, one step at a time. *Walk, just walk.* But her shoes refused to move across the slippery, sugared floor.

She took a deep breath and closed the distance between the line and the blond in a matter of seconds. She drew within arm's length, admiring the way his hair curled over the collar of his polo shirt. The colors, blue and gold, looked familiar, almost like the shirt the staff had worn for a youth retreat last summer.

Lori's hand reached out to tap his shoulder, then hovered in midair. It *was* the same polo shirt. And that long hair curling over the man's ears also looked more than a little familiar. "Andy?" Her voice squeaked.

Andy turned in his seat to face her, surprise covering his features. "Lori! What are you doing here? Needed a sugar fix?" He rose from his chair with a grin.

"I'm, uh… Actually, I was just…" Her voice trailed off. "What are *you* doing here?"

His cheeks pinked, and he shuffled his feet. "Meeting someone."

Lori's stomach pinched. Not another date. She chewed on her lower lip, almost unwilling to ask the question hovering in her mouth. "Eva?"

"What? No!" Andy cleared his throat. "I mean, no. It's a blind date."

Lori blinked twice. "A blind date?"

"I know that's lame. Two in one week."

It couldn't be—but it was. Haley had set her and Andy up. Disappointment filled Lori's senses, then relief. At least she wouldn't be forced to make small talk with a complete stranger.

But now the hope of meeting her secret admirer was also gone. How dare Haley do this to her? Though she supposed it was a decent prank. Anger mixed with amusement, and Lori choked out a laugh.

"It's not that funny, is it?"

"No, you don't understand. I'm supposed to be on a blind date, too."

"Oh." A momentary shadow crossed Andy's face, and then realization brightened his eyes. "Oh!"

"We've been tricked." Lori *tsked* with her tongue.

"I never even saw it coming." Andy shook his head. "I'm slipping."

"Or maybe the kids are just getting good."

"Maybe so." Andy tilted his head, his gaze lingering on hers. "Why don't we go ahead and get a beignet while we're here? It'd be a shame to waste the opportunity."

"Excellent point."

"Want to get it to go, and sit outside somewhere?"

"Sure." Another measure of relief washed over Lori. At least outside it wouldn't feel quite so much like a date.

They rejoined the to-go line to order, Lori's heart thudding painfully the entire time. Standing behind Andy, she drew a tight breath as the scent of his familiar cologne stirred up another round of the feelings she kept trying to bury. She mentally kicked herself. Technically, this was no different than any other time she and Andy had come here together. But with the weight of Haley's manipulation hanging over their heads, it sure felt different.

She was definitely going to have a word or two with that skinny little blonde.

"Hey, look. Our table is open." Andy gestured toward the corner of the patio. "Let's sit there instead."

Lori's eyebrows rose with surprise. He thought of it as their spot, too. She wanted to insist they eat outside where the busy

French Quarter traffic could distract from this weird feeling in her stomach, but Andy was already hurrying toward the vacant table. Reluctantly, Lori left the line and followed him across the floor.

She took a seat and focused on looping her purse over the back of the chair so it wouldn't get coated with sugar from the floor. Andy's fingers drummed a fast beat on the tabletop. They looked at each, smiled, looked away, back, and then burst into simultaneous laughter.

"Wow, this is awkward. I'm sorry." Andy exhaled loudly.

"It's not your fault." Lori tossed back her hair and smiled. "Haley's really going to get it for this one, isn't she?"

"I'm thinking snack duty at church for life." Andy laughed. "But, hey, it got us here, and we needed a chance to catch up. I feel like I haven't really talked to you in forever. I barely saw you at the Wednesday-night service."

"The kids kept me busy, and with Summer there…" Lori's voice trailed off. She knew the excuse sounded petty, but she couldn't admit that ever since that near kiss, being around Andy was sometimes more painful than pleasant. That would ruin their friendship for sure.

Andy cleared his throat. "I've missed you."

Lori swallowed. "I—I've missed you, too." Her heart hammered, but doubt tickled the fringes of her mind. He couldn't mean it the way she hoped. He probably meant he missed all their joking around or ragging on her many shoe purchases— not that he missed her, personally. If that was the case, he would have kissed her when he had the chance last weekend.

Mercifully, a waitress came then and took their order, and minutes later whisked back with plates of beignets and two cups of coffee.

Lori shoved a piece of beignet in her mouth, and instantly her stress eased. Too bad there wasn't any chocolate syrup to drizzle on top. At least filling her mouth saved her from having to say anything else about missing Andy.

Andy bit into his pastry. "So, how did Summer like the youth service?"

"She enjoyed it. She's excited about the retreat." Lori forked another piece of beignet from her plate.

"The kids seemed to take to her well."

"I knew they would."

Andy sipped at his coffee and then paused. "I have a question. Might sound stupid, but I have to ask."

Lori nibbled on her lower lip, having a sinking feeling she knew where the conversation was heading. *Please don't be about us, please don't be about us.*

"Are you mad at me?" The vulnerability in Andy's gaze nearly tore out Lori's heart.

She busied herself with brushing her sugary fingers on a napkin. "Why do you ask?" He had to be referring to her distance at the shop, but Lori couldn't admit to being frustrated without starting an argument. This nondate was awkward enough without adding a fight to the mix. Or maybe he was referring to the taboo topic of last weekend's movie night. Either way, not something she was up for discussing.

"Every time I see you lately, you seem upset."

Lori played with the crumbs on her plate. "I didn't realize."

"Lori, come on. Be honest with me." Andy scooted his plate aside and leaned forward.

She stared at her coffee cup, unwilling to meet his eyes. "I guess maybe I am a little upset." She drew a deep breath. "So, now I have a question for you." *No, don't go there. Stop talking.* But Lori's mouth wouldn't listen to her mind. "Are you checking up on me for your aunt? Is that why you're always popping in the store and asking me about business and profits at church?"

Andy lifted one corner of his mouth in a half smile. "Busted."

"You really are?" Lori shouldn't have been surprised, but she was a little shocked that he admitted it so freely.

"Yes. Bella asked me to keep it a secret. She was worried

about your finding out and losing confidence in yourself. She didn't want you getting paranoid about managing the shop. She just wanted me to keep an eye on things. To be there in case you needed help." Andy released a heavy sigh.

"Did you not think I could do the job?" Hurt laced Lori's tone, and she couldn't help but frown.

"Of course I thought you could—*knew* you could," Andy corrected. "But I couldn't turn down my aunt. She was already stressed about her family, and she needed to be able to relax and not worry about the store."

"I guess I can understand that." Lori fingered the edge of her coffee cup. "Have you been giving her good reports?"

"Yes, because you've been doing a great job." Andy's brow furrowed. "Hopefully she won't be too upset that I told you."

"I won't tell if you won't." Lori smiled, glad the truth no longer stood between them. At least now Andy wouldn't have to pretend to be asking from his own interest, and she wouldn't have to wonder if he believed in her capabilities.

"So you're not mad?"

"No. I'm not mad." She narrowed her eyes playfully. "I do think that this calls for another beignet, though, your treat."

"Coming right up." Andy ran his fingers through his hair as he scooted his chair back, then noticed the sugar on his hands. He patted at his head. "Uh-oh. How bad is it?"

"Let's just say I didn't realize you were going gray before your time." Lori winked.

"Very funny. Help me get it out, would you?" He leaned forward, and Lori reached to brush the powder from the fine blond strands.

Andy's eyes met hers, and his grin faded to a more serious expression, their faces close together. "Lori, listen. There's something you should know."

Lori flicked at another lock of his hair, frowning slightly at the glazed powder refusing to budge. "What's that?"

His mouth opened, but before he could speak, Lori's gaze locked on something over his shoulder. A man with a thin goatee and wire-rim glasses heading toward their table. No. It couldn't be. But the green eyes behind those familiar black frames flickered to meet hers, and she knew it was.

Her fingers curled into Andy's hair.

"Hey!" he yelped and pulled backward, rubbing his head. "What was that for?"

"Him." She couldn't breathe.

"Him who?" Andy twisted in his seat. "Who is that?" Andy's eyes darted back and forth between the tall, distinguished-looking man approaching their table and Lori.

He was back. Jason was back in town. *Her* town. Lori clenched her fists on the table. Her knees felt weak, and not from being swept off her feet as Jason had once done. No, this time it was out of sheer indignation. She gritted her teeth.

"Who is that?" Andy asked again. Lori's mouth opened to answer, but at that moment Jason grinned at her, and she snapped it closed again. She struggled to keep her shock in check as Jason stopped at their table.

"Lori. It's good to see you again."

Andy rose from his chair and offered his hand. "Andy Stewart. And you are?"

He shook Andy's hand, but his eyes never left Lori. Her stomach twisted. "Jason Chumley."

Andy's expression contorted to mirror what Lori was sure resembled her own, and his fists doubled. No doubt he was re-membering everything Lori had ever told him about her ex—which was a lot.

"What are you doing here?" Lori finally found her voice, proud of the sharp edge it carried. No sense hiding her feelings.

Jason looked undisturbed. "Getting a beignet, what else?" His wide smile stretched, so fake it seemed plastic. Too bad she hadn't seen through him years ago.

"I mean, what are you doing in New Orleans?" Lori stood as well, determined to hold her ground. Andy looked as though he'd love to take a swing at Jason, and at the moment, Lori wasn't sure she'd stop him.

"I'd hoped to have this conversation elsewhere." Jason's voice lowered, and his gaze darted to Andy, then back. Good. Let him be nervous.

"What conversation?" Lori crossed her arms over her chest. "I don't have anything to say to you."

Jason drew a deep breath, his smile slightly wavering. "Rightly so. However…" He cleared his throat. "I came to New Orleans to find you."

"Why would—" Lori's eyes widened as reality struck like a blow to her gut. "It was you." A fresh wave of shock nearly knocked her off balance. The timing was perfect. It all made sense now—horrible, perfect sense. Her hand clutched at the neckline of her shirt in protection of her heart. "You sent the gifts, didn't you? You're my secret admirer."

"Of course I am." Jason's smile was back, wider than ever, and his eyes warmed as Lori's hopes froze. "Who else would it be?"

# *Chapter Sixteen*

Friday night, Lori snuggled on the couch with an oversized pillow in her lap, a chocolate bar in one hand and a white chocolate mocha in the other. Her mind had yet to process the shock of seeing Jason earlier in the day. She'd worked through a mindless afternoon at the shop, came home and, before she even prayed for it, found a message from Gracie on her answering machine. Her friend had announced she was home, unpacked and wanting to come over for the evening.

Now Gracie sat facing Lori on the other end of the sofa, feet propped on the cushion Lori held and her own flavored coffee in hand.

"Chocolate, caffeine and cashmere socks." Gracie wiggled her blue-socked feet in Lori's lap. "Everything a girl needs to dish. Now, spill it. I want to hear everything. You sounded so panicked on the phone."

"You should tell me about your honeymoon first." She wasn't stalling—exactly. She just wasn't sure how to start. Lori sipped her coffee and let the hot liquid warm her all the way through. But the chill of seeing Jason again wouldn't go away.

"Are you kidding?" Gracie shook her red hair back from her face and smiled. "Okay, fine. The honeymoon was perfect.

Lots of alone time, gorgeous scenery and more seafood than I could ever hope to eat again. Your turn. What's up?"

Lori drew a deep breath and stared at the plastic lid on her cup. Might as well blurt it out. "I ran into Jason today at Café Du Monde."

Gracie's eyes widened. "Jason Chumley? The guy who cheated on you? Your Jason?"

Lori nodded. "The very one." But he wasn't hers anymore. Not by a long shot.

Gracie sat back against the couch, her jaw set. "Let Carter have a word or two with him. I'm sure he'd be happy to communicate how you feel."

"I know he would. You married a good one." Lori smiled wistfully. "But in this case, that wouldn't be wise."

Gracie studied her friend through narrowed eyes. "You're leaving something out, aren't you?" Her nails tapped a rhythm on her coffee cup.

"Just a small detail." Lori laughed, but it came out hollow and hard. "He's sort of my secret admirer."

"What?" Gracie sat up so fast she jostled Lori's coffee. "That's impossible."

"Why? It makes sense, in a twisted way." Lori took a bite of her chocolate bar, willing her endorphins to work their magic. "Think about it. All the personal details of those gifts meant it was someone who knew me really well. And who knows me better than the guy I dated and was engaged to for years?"

"I refuse to believe it." Gracie set her cup on the coffee table and crossed her arms.

"What do you mean? He said so himself."

Gracie blinked rapidly, then shook her head. "Again, impossible."

"Why are you so sure it's not him?" Lori closed the wrapper on her candy bar and tossed it on the pillow with a huff. Gracie hadn't even been around the last month, and now suddenly she was an expert on Lori's secret admirer? Gracie hadn't even seen the gifts. "You're being weird."

"It almost sounds like you want your secret admirer to be Jason—which is what's weird, if you ask me." Gracie raised her eyebrows at Lori.

They stared at each other, each refusing to back down, as the clock above the sofa loudly ticked away the seconds. Slowly, Lori let her shoulders relax as she eased back against the cushions. How many times had she and Gracie argued on this very couch? About men, money, friendships. Until now, she hadn't realized exactly how much she'd missed her old roommate.

"Listen, I don't want to fight." Lori broke the chocolate bar in half and handed Gracie the bigger piece with a smile. "Truce?"

"Truce. Keep your chocolate, you need it more than me." Gracie grinned; then her expression slowly sobered. "But please explain why you're defending Jason."

"I'm not defending him—and I didn't want him to be my secret admirer, trust me. I couldn't have picked a worse person for that title." Lori shuddered. "But these gifts are different than his usual style—which might mean that he's changed." That fact had dawned on Lori during her afternoon at work and had erased the top layer of her anger. She would never consider dating Jason again, but if he was searching for forgiveness, she could possibly offer him that much—if he was sincere. With Jason, it was always hard to tell.

Gracie started shaking her head again. "I don't think—"

Lori interrupted. "The last present was a monogrammed Bible cover. When did Jason ever do anything remotely spiritual before?"

"He didn't." Gracie paused. "But supposedly sending that Bible cover doesn't necessarily mean he's changed now."

"There's no *supposedly* about it. It was him. He said so himself. Andy was my witness."

Gracie's face suddenly turned red, and she coughed hard, pounding herself on the chest.

"Are you okay? Here, drink." Lori handed her the cup she'd placed on the coaster earlier.

Gracie took a sip, and her natural color returned, but she kept her eyes averted. "Sorry, got choked up there."

"On what?"

"Never mind. You were saying?" Gracie cleared her throat and took another sip of coffee.

Apparently that Mexican sun had gotten to her friend. Lori peeled back the wrapper on her chocolate, wishing it was one of the signature gators from the shop instead of the store-bought candy she'd found in her newly supplied emergency stash at home. "I said Andy was with me at Café Du Monde when Jason showed up, so he heard his confession, too."

"Andy was there." Gracie pressed her fingers to her lips.

"Yes."

"Andy was there when Jason admitted to being your secret admirer."

"Yes!" Lori fought a wave of impatience. Was Gracie losing it? How many times did she have to repeat herself?

"And he said nothing? Nothing at all?"

"No, why would he?"

Gracie closed her eyes for a brief moment, as if gathering her thoughts. "I'm just surprised, that's all. I figured Andy would have something to say. He knows about your past with Jason, and he's a good friend. That's all."

Lori shrugged. "I think it surprised both of us, to be honest. We never saw it coming."

"I bet," Gracie mumbled.

"Are you okay?" Lori frowned.

Gracie rubbed her temples with both fingers. "Fine. Must be the jet lag." She let out a sigh that sounded more frustrated than tired.

"So, do you believe me now about Jason? Since Andy heard him say it?"

"I guess I have to." Gracie didn't exactly look thrilled, but at least she wasn't arguing.

Lori downed the rest of her coffee and swung her legs over the side of the couch. "I'm not saying I'm not disappointed."

Hope lit Gracie's eyes "You are?"

"Why is me being disappointed good news?" Lori wrinkled her forehead.

"It's not, of course. I'm just happy you're not excited about Jason being your admirer."

This was getting confusing. No wonder Gracie was rubbing her head as if she had a headache. Lori felt the sudden strong urge to do the same. She rotated her neck on her shoulders. "I'm glad I know who the secret admirer is, but I wish it wasn't Jason. I really was hoping to meet Mr. Right this way." And she had really wanted Mr. Right to be the one man it could never be—Andy. A grim taste filled her mouth.

Gracie offered a sympathetic smile. "Your turn will come."

"I know. I guess." Lori nudged Gracie with her shoulder and smiled. "I really am happy for you guys. I don't mean to sound bitter."

"You'll find that same happiness soon, I can feel it." Gracie looped her arm around Lori's shoulders. "Was there someone you were hoping the gifts would be from?"

Lori paused as Andy's face again flashed in her mind. She took one look at Gracie's open, searching gaze and swallowed hard. "Nope. No one in particular."

Guy night—finally. Was anything better than hanging out with an old friend, watching sports on TV and drinking a ridiculous amount of Dr Pepper? Andy crinkled the empty aluminum can in his hand, then tossed it across the room to Carter. "Heads up!"

Carter caught the can and rebounded it into the trash can by the TV. "Nothing but net!"

Andy cranked the handle on the recliner, propping his feet up. "Do me a favor, man. Don't get married and leave for a month again."

"I don't plan on it." Carter fisted another handful of popcorn into his mouth. "Weddings are expensive." He laughed.

Andy grinned. Lucky for him, Gracie and Lori declared an emergency girl-talk night. That left him and Carter to catch up on their trip, eat some junk food and, most importantly, get Andy's mind off Lori. He relaxed against the soft cushions of the recliner and tried to clear his thoughts. He couldn't believe Jason had showed up out of nowhere and stolen Andy's credit for the gifts. He'd been so shocked that he couldn't deny it, and by the time he found his voice, it was too late. The lie had progressed.

The worst part was Lori hadn't seemed too bothered by it.

The front door of Gracie and Carter's new house suddenly slammed. Andy jumped, heart hammering in his throat. Across the room, Carter's face scrunched. "Uh-oh. Three, two…"

"Are you crazy?" Gracie burst around the corner of the entryway, temper as fiery as her red hair. Her hands planted on her hips, she stared at Andy until he squirmed against the leather upholstery. "You stood right there and didn't say anything while another man claimed your work? And your woman?"

Andy attempted to stand, but the chair threw him off balance, and he fell back against the seat. "First of all, Lori's not mine, which is the whole point."

Gracie sagged against the door frame and crossed her arms. "She could have been if you had spoken up."

"You assume." Andy looked to Carter for help, but his friend simply held up both hands in refusal.

"Why on earth would you not correct Jason? He had the nerve to lie to her face, and you let him?" Gracie shook her head, and her hair bounced. "I don't understand."

"You didn't see Lori's expression." Andy struggled to his feet and faced off with Gracie. "You didn't see that little smile after that jerk said what he did." He rubbed his hands down the length of his cheeks and sighed. "She seemed happy it was him. I didn't want to mess that up."

Gracie opened her mouth, then closed it. She opened it again, looked over at Carter and then back at Andy. She threw her hands in the air. "I can't say anything to her without betraying you. Do you have any idea how frustrating this is? All because you can't be honest with her about your feelings."

"I'm not so sure what I feel anymore." Andy slowly sank back onto the recliner. He'd thought his friendship with Lori had found solid footing again and had planned on breaking the news about the gifts at Café Du Monde during their impromptu date—until Jason showed up and ruined everything. Now he had no idea where he stood.

Gracie moved to sit beside Carter on the couch, tugging a blue plaid throw pillow into her lap. She inhaled slowly. "Do you love Lori?"

Andy stared at his hands. It really was too soon to admit something like that, especially to someone other than Lori. But he couldn't lie; he'd known Gracie for years, and she'd see right through him, just like she always did. He licked his dry lips. "Yes."

"So you want what's best for her?"

Andy looked up in surprise. "Always."

"And you really think that's Jason?" Gracie wound her arm around Carter's and leaned against his shoulder. Her face nestled perfectly against his arm, as if they were two puzzle pieces cut to fit.

A lump knotted in Andy's throat. Was Lori his matching piece, his other half? Or was he wishing for something that would never be? Surely her puzzle piece wasn't Jason, not after the horrible way he'd treated her.

But the choice wasn't his to make. Until Lori showed him that Jason still didn't claim a portion of her heart after all these years, he would have to stay out of the picture.

Andy leaned forward, bracing his elbows against his knees, and looked Gracie square on. "I think that's up to Lori to decide."

Gracie squirmed as if she wanted to say more, but didn't argue. Of course, the hand Carter laid on her arm could have been a warning to hush. "Fine. That's your call. I just think you're making a big mistake."

"You're not going to tell her about the gifts, are you?" Panic seized Andy's stomach, and the sausage pizza he and Carter had ordered twisted like a rope of licorice. "You can't."

Gracie's chin lifted. "I won't lie for you."

"I'm not asking you to lie. I'm asking you not to volunteer information that isn't any of your business." Andy struggled to keep his voice firm when all he wanted to do was drop to his knees and beg Gracie to keep quiet.

"All right." She blew at a piece of hair that fell across her forehead. "But I still think you're making a big—"

"A big mistake. I know, I know." Andy sighed, turning to look out the picture window at the growing darkness. "You're not the only one."

## Chapter Seventeen

Saturday-morning business was at an all-time high. Lori didn't even take time to break for lunch between the steady streams of customers. Apparently everyone in the city was celebrating the beautiful weekend with chocolate and coffee.

"Monny, what's the status on that raspberry-swirl cake?" Lori called over her shoulder as he bustled through the kitchen door with a fresh supply of chocolate-dipped marshmallows. She counted change for a customer and smiled. "Have a nice day."

Summer intercepted Monny and took the heavy silver tray from his hands. "Thank you, *mi cara*." He brushed his hands together and started back toward the kitchen. "Cake will be ready in ten."

He disappeared into the kitchen while Lori slid open the display case and Summer deposited the desserts inside. "Thanks." She shut the case as Lori turned back to the register. "Today is crazy. I don't think I've taken a breath yet."

"Just wait until next week." Lori closed the register drawer with a bang. "Valentine's Day will be even worse. And with it falling on a Sunday this year, everyone will be shopping for treats the Friday and Saturday before."

"Are we going to run another sale?" Summer leaned one hip against the counter and studied her chipped black nail polish.

"I'm not sure yet." Lori swatted at Summer. "And hey, no touching the glass. I just cleaned that this morning."

"Aye, aye, Boss." Summer moved away from the display and glanced around the store. "Looks like we finally have a lull. What do you need me to do next?"

Lori fought to keep the shock from her expression. Summer, volunteering for more work? She really had changed over these last few weeks. Ever since Lori had confided in her about the blunder with Monny, Summer's production at work had increased. It seemed like the girl had just been bored before— apparently, a new friend made all the difference. Summer seemed a far cry from the sullen, moody student who barely lifted a finger and routinely dressed all in black.

Lori studied Summer's long-sleeve black top, dark denim jeans and black cropped jacket. Well, she was still wearing black, but not for long. She smiled. "You can wipe down those vacant tables over there. But first, I have a surprise. Sort of a gimmick to promote Valentine's Day."

"Oh, yeah? What?"

Lori hurried into the supply room off the kitchen and came back with a cardboard box. "Hand me those scissors over there, please."

Summer passed over the blue-handled scissors, and Lori cut into the packing tape. "I ordered these last week. They just got here yesterday." Yesterday Lori hadn't been anywhere near the right frame of mind to do anything but make it through the afternoon, much less care about a delivery. She set the scissors on the counter and pulled open the box flaps. In retrospect, today shouldn't be any better. Nothing had changed from the day before. But at least with the shop so busy, she could distract herself from thinking about Jason.

And Andy's lack of response at Café Du Monde. He had puffed

up at Jason's arrival, but after the revealing of her secret admirer, Andy deflated faster than a balloon at a child's birthday party.

Lori's stomach twisted, and before she could sink into a bad mood, she hurriedly lifted two aprons from the box. "Ta-da!" She held one at her waist to model for Summer. They turned out cuter than Lori had hoped, with the pink background and black trim. *The Chocolate Gator* was stitched across the front in a black cursive font. It was just the thing to draw attention and cheer up the place for the coming holiday.

Summer's eyes widened in alarm. "Those are pink."

"*And* black." Lori tossed Summer's apron to her. "Tie it on."

"You've got to be kidding. Can't I just clean the bathrooms instead?" Summer held the apron as far away from her as she could, as if it might bite.

"You'll be doing that later, too." Lori laughed. "Come on, it's not so bad."

"Monny doesn't have to wear one." Summer pouted.

"Monny's in the kitchen, isn't usually seen by customers and actually gets his aprons dirty. These are for show." Lori looped the ties around her waist and straightened the front. "See? Cute. You can wear it over your usual work clothes."

"Great," Summer grumbled. "Why not stick me in some high heels while you're at it?" She tied her apron with quick, jerky movements and moved to stand in front of the display counter's reflection. "Pink. I'm wearing pink."

"Live a little. You might actually like it." Lori playfully hip-checked her.

Summer stumbled to one side but continued to stare glumly at her image. "I doubt that."

"It softens you up. Maybe you'll catch yourself a man." Lori stuffed the bubble wrap inside the box and folded the cardboard flaps back down. Several of the youth-group members' older brothers had sure looked interested last Wednesday when they came to pick up their siblings after the service. Summer, however, remained either oblivious or aloof to the fact.

"Why bother? You've got more than enough men for both of us." The teasing light returned to Summer's eyes. "Which one would you rather share?"

Lori paused, hands lingering on the package. "What are you talking about?"

"Jason. Andy. This secret admirer of yours…" Summer's voice trailed off as she ticked the names on her fingers.

Lori shook her head. "Jason isn't mine, and neither is Andy. And, as it turns out, my secret admirer *is* Jason."

"Really?" Summer frowned. "You didn't mention that little detail yesterday afternoon when you said you ran into your ex."

"I wasn't exactly in a detailed type of mood then."

"I remember, trust me." Summer rolled her eyes. "Well, hey, if wearing this apron makes you happy, I'll do it. Anything is better than Ms. Grumpy from yesterday."

"Thanks, I think." Lori wrinkled her nose and handed Summer the delivery box. "Will you take this back to the supply room for me? We might be able to use it later."

Summer obediently headed toward the supply room, shaking her apron-clad hips with exaggeration.

"Ha ha," Lori called after her. She turned as the bell over the door rang. A uniformed deliveryman strolled inside, a small package clutched under one arm.

"Delivery for Ms. Perkins." He set the box on the counter.

"That's me." Another delivery from her secret admirer? Lori's heart rate spiked until she remembered Jason was the culprit. Her smile slowly faded.

"This was sent a few days ago. It fell behind the seat in my truck." He adjusted his baseball cap. "Sorry about that. Sign here."

"No problem—it happens." Lori scrawled her name on the electronic signature pad. "Thanks."

"Have a nice day."

As the deliveryman walked back outside to his truck, she tore open the package and pulled out a small pink gift box tied with a red bow.

"Another gift?" Summer hurried across the shop and leaned her elbows against the counter despite Lori's previous warning about the clean glass.

"This one was sent several days ago. The truck driver misplaced it."

Summer tilted her head to one side. "I wonder why Jason mailed it this time instead of delivering it through the random people like before."

Lori quirked an eyebrow. "Maybe because you yelled at an old lady and I got stuck in a window?" Which meant Jason must have been lurking nearby, watching the entire ordeal. Her cheeks flushed in embarrassment.

"Oh, yeah." Summer's face darkened, and she cleared her throat. "Hurry up! Open it."

Lori ripped into the paper and pulled out a stack of polka-dotted stationery and sticky notes tied together with a straw ribbon. A plain note card nestled between the strings with a typed message.

*My Lori—*

*To the woman who makes more lists than anyone I've ever known—just one of your many adorable qualities. Here's a supply to get you through the next few pro/con situations.*

*Love,*
*Your Secret Admirer*

A knot lumped in Lori's throat at the sweet words. She tried to picture Jason pounding out this message at a typewriter or computer but couldn't. It made sense, though—he definitely had been victim of her pro/con lists over the years. He even used to tease Lori about them, to the point where she started making them in secret. Was this Jason's way of apologizing for the past, of showing her he'd changed and wanted her forgiveness?

"What's it say?" Summer craned her head, trying to read the small type.

Silently, Lori handed over the card.

"Wow, pretty good stuff." Summer tossed the note card on the counter. "What a romantic."

"I guess." Lori fingered the edges of the card. Jason never had been romantic before. But then again, he always did know how to get what he wanted. Was this another ploy? Or a gift from his heart?

No one could answer such questions on an empty stomach. "I need chocolate." Lori pulled open the glass case and claimed a chocolate crocodile from a lace doily. She bit off the gator's head and pretended not to notice Summer snatching a piece from the display for herself.

The chocolate melted slowly in Lori's mouth. But she could probably eat everything in the store and still not have enough clarity to solve this issue. She needed advice from someone who knew her as well as Jason, but wasn't biased like Gracie. Someone who'd heard the entire story but remained a neutral party.

She needed Andy.

Andy's cell phone lit inside the cup holder of the movie-theater chair. He glanced at the number on the display screen, and his eyes widened. Lori's number. He quickly pulled the cell free, grateful he remembered to put it on mute before taking some of his youth to see a new family-friendly comedy, and flipped it open. "Hold on just a second," he said softly.

He leaned over the armrest and whispered to Jeremy, "I have to take this. I'll be right back." Then he stood and stumbled past the jeans-clad legs of his protesting youth group. He finally cleared the aisle and hurried into the lobby of the theater. "Are you there?"

"Yes." Lori's soft voice made his stomach flip. "Where are you?"

"Today was movie day, remember? It was on the church calendar." Andy dodged a young mother chasing after her two toddlers and headed toward the restrooms, where it was less chaotic. The scent of buttered popcorn wafted from the refreshment stand, and he wished Lori were here so he'd have an excuse to share a bag with her again.

"That's right. I almost forgot." Lori sighed, her breath whooshing through the phone. "I feel so out of touch with the youth lately, ever since taking on this new job."

"I would imagine." Andy ached to tell Lori exactly how much he missed her but bit back the words. It wasn't his right—not until she figured out things with Jason. The very thought of that jerk's name made Andy lose his appetite, and he turned his back to the refreshment stand.

"I didn't realize you were at a movie. Go back in with the kids—we can talk later."

Was it his imagination or did Lori sound disappointed? Andy fought the hope rising in his throat and tried to keep his voice nonchalant. "It's no problem. This particular movie isn't exactly a brainteaser. I can miss a few scenes. What's up?"

"I wanted to talk about Jason."

His hopes plummeted toward the gum stuck on the baseboard of the theater wall. So much for positive thinking. He pinched the bridge of his nose between his fingers. "Oh?"

"I'm confused." Lori blew out her breath in a huff. "He shows up out of nowhere, sending me these gifts—probably buttering me up before letting me know he's back. I don't know what to do."

*He's lying to you.* Andy longed to scream the words into the phone but pressed his lips together instead. It wasn't his place.

At this point, putting himself into the equation would only add to Lori's stress and confusion. Until she worked out her feelings about Jason, Andy had to stay out of it.

Even if that did mean spending Valentine's Day alone with a TV dinner, wondering how much longer he'd have a job.

"Andy? Are you there?" Lori's voice jerked him away from his dark thoughts and back to his equally dark reality.

"I'm here." He forced a smile, hoping it would show in his voice.

"Another gift came today."

"It did?" Andy paused, hoping he hadn't sounded too shocked. He hadn't sent any gifts in days. Did Jason decide to suddenly start sending his own presents in order to give merit to his lie?

"Yeah, the delivery driver almost lost the package. It was dated several days ago. Stationery with my initials printed on the front, and a really sweet note." Lori's voice softened. "It was very romantic. You should read it."

No need. Andy had every word memorized. He had, after all, labored over what to write for at least half an hour. He balled his fist and pounded the carpeted theater wall soundlessly with one hand. "I'll have to do that."

"It sounded nothing like Jason. Maybe he really has changed. He never was the romantic type."

Or the loyal type, from what Lori had told him before. Andy slowly leaned forward and rested his forehead against the poster of an upcoming movie, not sure how much longer he could stand this conversation. "Mmm-hmm."

"I'm sorry to keep you from the movie. I just wanted your opinion." Lori suddenly sounded lost, and her confusion nearly broke Andy's heart. "You know about my past with Jason, and you're my best friend. What should I do?"

*Dump him. Marry me.* Andy briefly closed his eyes, afraid to open his mouth lest the words jump out on their own accord.

"Andy?"

"I'd say pray about it." He winced at the trite-sounding answer, but the meaning was sincere. "Definitely pray about it before making any big decisions."

At this point, only God could clear up the mess Andy had made.

## Chapter Eighteen

Lori stood, arms crossed against the unseasonably cold wind, staring blindly down the bustling French Quarter street. Pray about it? That's all her youth-minister-best-friend could say? It's not like she hadn't already prayed about it, and she knew prayer should be a first resort, not the last—but surely Andy could have contributed something else. Something logical, practical. Something with feeling.

Something like *Forget about Jason and fall in love with me*.

The wind tickled the hair at Lori's neck, and she flipped up the collar of her red plaid coat. Andy wasn't interested in her that way; he'd made that clearer than the glass on the display counter in the shop. If he had ever thought of her as more than a best friend, he wouldn't have dismissed her plea for help so callously. So why did her thoughts keep going there? It appeared, for whatever reason, that Jason was suddenly wedging his way back into her life—while Andy seemed to be trying to wiggle out.

With a frustrated sigh, Lori dropped her cell in her coat pocket and turned toward the shop. The sound of her name being shouted against the wind made her turn at the door.

"Lori." Jason jogged down the sidewalk, his cheeks bright

red in the cold winter air. He looked the same as always—wire-rim glasses, simple but classy black jacket, designer dress slacks even on a Saturday. He appeared wealthy, sophisticated, intelligent. One would never look at him and imagine he'd cheat on his fiancée months before their wedding.

The memory steeled Lori's spine, and she kept one hand on the chilly door handle. Inside, Summer looked up from wiping down a table and made a surprised *O* with her mouth as her eyes caught Lori's. She straightened slowly, rag in hand, and gestured outside with raised eyebrows. Lori shook her head. No, she didn't need backup. She could handle Jason on her own.

After Andy's brush-off, apparently she was going to have to.

She struggled to keep her expression neutral, trying to remember Jason had changed, had sent those romantic gifts that just days ago had given her a new hope for the future. She wouldn't tell him off just yet. A relationship was out of the question, but forgiving him might not be, if he proved himself. Jaw clenched, she forced a smile. "What do you want?"

His easy grin didn't falter. "I wanted to see you. We didn't get to talk very long at Café Du Monde." He paused. "Were you on a date?"

"With Andy? No, he's just a friend." *Thanks for rubbing it in.* Lori welcomed the distraction of a streetcar driving past, grateful she had somewhere to look for a moment other than into Jason's intense gaze.

"Good to hear." His stance relaxed, and he shoved his hands into his coat pockets. "I'd hate to think I came all this way for nothing."

Lori's heart jerked. "What are you talking about?"

"I told you I came to see you."

His saying so didn't make it true. Then again, there were the gifts…. Lori released her breath in a slow sigh. "Thanks for the presents. They were thoughtful."

A quick shadow flashed across Jason's face, then was gone

so fast Lori wondered if it had really happened. "Anytime. I knew you'd like them." He cleared his throat. "Listen, I was wondering if you'd accompany me to dinner. We obviously need to talk."

Lori hedged. Gifts or not, could she sit across a table from the man who broke her heart and destroyed her self-esteem with one really bad, really embarrassing choice? She'd been the talk of their church for weeks, the victim of pitying looks and awkward pats on the back. She shuddered at the recollection.

"I want to apologize. Officially."

Lori evaluated his gaze, searching for sincerity or a secret motive. What would be so bad about an apology dinner? She deserved at least that much from Jason after the way he'd treated her. She could order something expensive and chocolaty, accept his apology and put this secret-admirer stuff behind her once and for all. She could move on and put her full focus on the Chocolate Gator. Maybe she'd even write up a business proposal and apply for that loan she'd mentioned to Summer.

A crowd of tourists in family-reunion T-shirts suddenly pushed past them on the sidewalk, jostling Lori's purse and her thoughts. She had to make a decision now. No time for a pro/con list. She stepped out of the way to let the rest of the crowd pass and met Jason's eyes briefly. "Sure. Just tell me when and where."

One dinner to make him go away. What could it hurt?

Lori doubted her decision the second she left the Chocolate Gator and headed toward Decatur Street. The uncertainty didn't stop even as she stepped through the rust-colored doors of Café Maspero and breathed in the smell of fresh bread, browned meat and olives. Her stomach grumbled, but she didn't think it was from hunger—most likely it was from seeing Jason raise his hand and gesture to her from a table in the back.

She took a fortifying breath and wove through the maze of

wooden tables, under the bricked archway and past a sea of red-upholstered chairs. She must be crazy for agreeing to meet Jason for dinner. Her justification of ordering an expensive meal couldn't even be carried out here, since Café Maspero was known for their great prices and huge portions.

Lori paused at the table across from Jason and didn't return his smile. "I changed my mind."

His welcoming grin faded, and he slowly stood. "Lori, please. Just hear me out. You're already here, and I know you must be hungry from working all day. Sit." He sank back onto his chair and raised his eyebrows. "Please?"

Those muffalettas *did* smell good. Lori dropped her purse on the floor by her chair and sat. "Fine. But make it fast."

He handed her a menu. "This place is amazing. I've already been twice since arriving in the city. No wonder you love New Orleans so much. Did you know this restaurant site used to be a slave exchange? *And* the same place where Andrew Jackson plotted the New Orleans battle?"

Lori fought the urge to roll her eyes. Someone had obviously been hitting up the local guided tours. She snatched the menu from Jason's hands, then frowned. "Wait a minute. How long have you been in town?"

"The day before I found you at Café Du Monde. So, three days now."

Lori pretended to scan the limited menu, but her mind raced. If Jason had only been in town a few days, how had he sent the gifts these last two weeks?

"Are we ready to order?" A waitress hovered over their table with a notepad and pen.

Lori ordered a half muffaletta and water with lemon, and impatiently tapped her nails on the table as Jason requested the jambalaya and a Coke. The moment the waitress turned to leave, Lori leaned forward in accusation. "How did you know where I worked? Or that I was even still in New Orleans?"

Jason reached for her hand, but Lori moved it away. His expression turned to one of exasperation. "Lori, you grew up here. You always loved being a New Orleans native. I knew you weren't going anywhere."

She pulled in her lower lip, hating that he was right and still knew her that well. "I thought you moved back to Dallas after you…after we…" She couldn't even make herself say the words *cheated* or *broke up*.

"I've been back in Dallas for a few years, working for my father's consulting business." He made room for the waitress placing their drinks on the table, then turned his attention back to Lori. "I knew you'd still be in the city, so I did some sightseeing and asking around. I'd just found out from a girl at the aquarium that you were working temporarily at the Chocolate Gator when I ran into you at Café Du Monde."

Stupid old coworkers. Lori exhaled with a huff. She should have never called to update her friends in the gift shop and lobby about her new job. But then again, how was she supposed to know her ex-fiancé would track her down all the way from Texas?

Jason reached for her hand again. "It was fate."

Or a really, really bad cosmic joke.

"How did you end up working at the Chocolate Gator, anyway?"

Lori quickly picked up her water glass and took a sip, both to avoid his touch and to stall as she processed the dozens of questions threatening to pour from her mouth. So now she knew how Jason had found her in New Orleans—but what about Amy, the woman he'd left Lori for? Obviously they'd broken up if he'd hunted Lori down a full state away. But why now, after all these years? And what about the gifts?

"Lori?"

She blinked, struggling to focus on Jason's recent inquiry instead of her own. "What'd you ask? Oh, yeah—my friend's aunt owns the store. She needed a temporary fill-in while she visited family."

"I see. And you're enjoying it?"

Lori shrugged. "So far, but it's not my place. I'd love to open my own shoe or accessory store one day."

"You'd be amazing at that. You always had a head for business." Jason smiled.

"Apparently not." Lori snorted, thinking of all the disasters that had occurred so far at the Chocolate Gator. She didn't really seem to have a knack for anything anymore—except spending money she didn't have and picking out fantastic shoes.

"What do you mean, apparently not?"

"It doesn't matter." Lori crossed her arms over her chest, hating that she'd spilled so many of her personal dreams right there on the table to her ex. She narrowed her eyes. "How is it possible you sent the gifts if you've only been in New Orleans a few days? You just said you didn't even know where I worked until you got here."

Jason took a long sip of Coke and stirred the ice in his glass with his straw. "Doesn't it take the romance out of it if I explain every little detail?" He winked.

"No." She crossed her arms. "You're lying to me, aren't you?"

Jason sighed. "Yes, you caught me. I'm lying."

Lori's eyes widened. If he was lying, then who was her real secret admirer? Her hopes soared. This meant he was still out there somewhere, still penning his love, still planning romantic—

"I used my father's private investigator to find you weeks ago."

Lori's excitement collided with harsh reality. She fiddled with her straw, torn between wanting her admirer to be someone else—namely, Andy—and the hope that maybe Jason really had changed and was trying to prove it to her. But lying wasn't going to help. God, why can't my admirer be Mr. Right, instead of Mr. Almost-But-Never-Was?

Jason seemed to read her mind. "I'm sorry I lied. I just

didn't want to freak you out about the private-investigator thing. I don't want to scare you away."

Cheating on her months before their wedding had scared her away—not taking advantage of his father's flamboyant wealth by hiring someone to find her. Thankfully, the food arrived before Lori had a chance to respond, and she bit into her muffie with relief.

"Am I coming on too strong?" Jason wiped his mouth with his napkin and peered at her over the edge of his glasses in that familiar way he'd always done. "I just want you to know how sorry I am for the past. I'm trying to make it up to you."

Lori set her sandwich on her plate. "Look, I appreciate dinner and the apology, but I have a new life now. I'm happy." *Liar,* her conscience screamed. Well, she was trying to be happy, at least. Despite the fact she had no long-term career, no decent dating potentials and had gained four pounds the last time she'd stepped on the scale, thanks to her new easy access to chocolate crocodiles. "I don't understand why you're here."

"I thought it was obvious." Jason tilted his head to one side.

"You might want to spell it out for me." She refused to make it easy on him.

Jason removed his glasses and took her hand across the table. "I broke up with Amy not long after you and I split up. It was a mistake. I should have never treated you that way."

"No kidding." The mention of the other woman's name made Lori's fingers curl and her mind race. The memories. The lies. The broken dates. The late-night excuses as to why he never answered his phone. Lori abruptly tugged her hand free and grabbed her purse. "I knew I shouldn't have come." She fought a round of tears as she dug blindly for her wallet. Why had she let these long-buried emotions resurface? Jason had been as good as dead to her these last several years, and now he'd sprung back to the topsoil like a bad weed. If he wanted her forgiveness, he was going to have to try harder than that.

Jason shoved his full bowl away from him on the table and leaned forward in earnest. "The other day I was sitting in my high-rise office, surrounded by a ton of expensive, material things and I realized I didn't care about any of it. I miss you. What do I have to do to prove that to you?"

Lori wrestled a few bills free of her wallet and dropped the cash on the table as she stood. "You'll have to do a lot more than this." Then she turned on her heel and strode out the front door.

# Chapter Nineteen

Andy set the remaining two-liter drinks in the fridge and shut the door. Finally, the gym was cleaned up from the church's biannual potluck dinner. The youth group had volunteered—or, rather, Andy had volunteered the youth group—for cleanup duty this year instead of contributing food. A choice that, after tasting Jeremy and Haley's attempted cake last week, was probably wise.

Haley tossed the dishrag she'd been using to wipe the counters in the sink and brushed her hands on her jeans. "I'm beat."

"You?" Jeremy set his full bowl of leftover apple cobbler on the counter and flexed his bicep. "I'm the one who had to lug all those tables into the storage closet."

"Yeah, on a cart with *wheels*." Haley rolled her eyes.

"Don't start, you two," Andy warned. "I'm too tired to play referee." It'd be a long day of services, and thanks to the fresh onslaught of matchmaking attempts from the church's elder population and another not-so-subtle "get married" reminder from Pastor Mike, Andy hadn't been able to escape and go home until well after church ended. He'd grabbed lunch and had only been at his apartment for less than two hours before it was time to hurry back and lasso his youth group together for the evening service.

The fact that he hadn't heard from or seen Lori since their phone conversation at the movie theater yesterday didn't help. She hadn't shown up for church today or for the potluck. Andy kept shoveling green beans and ham casserole in his mouth, waiting for her to rush in with apologies for being late, but she never showed.

He couldn't think about how that might be because she was with Jason, or that casserole would make a not-so-grand reappearance.

"Don't worry, this isn't fighting. We're leaving, anyway." Haley tugged on Jeremy's sleeve. "Let's go. I've got homework tonight."

"See you Wednesday night, Pastor." Jeremy shrugged into his varsity football jacket, picked up his remaining dessert and then opened the gymnasium door for Haley. They waved and disappeared into the dark parking lot.

Andy made sure all the doors were locked, flipped off the overhead lights and dug his keys from his pants pocket. Finally, he could go home and crash—though dreams of Lori were sure to interrupt his sleep at this point. Maybe he'd watch a movie first and make some popcorn to settle that casserole roiling in his stomach. Deep down he knew it wasn't Widow Spencer's fault, though she might have overdone it with the peppers this time. It was his stress and paranoia over what Lori could be doing right now—and who she could be with.

He trudged toward his car, surprised to see Jeremy's truck still parked under the streetlight. Jeremy climbed out of the cab.

"My truck won't start." The teen shook his head. "It did this to me last week. I think it's the battery. Do you have any jumper cables?"

Andy winced. "Not anymore. Carter borrowed them before his wedding and I haven't gotten them back yet."

"Bummer." Jeremy spooned another bite of cobbler into his mouth. "Now what?"

Haley hopped out of the passenger side. "Room for two more, Pastor?"

"If you promise not to fight anymore." Andy gestured toward his car. "Let's go."

A few minutes later they were cruising down I-90 to Haley's house. Jeremy had kindly allowed Haley to have the front.

"So where was Lori tonight?" Haley's blond hair glowed in the light of the highway lamps as they flashed by.

Andy's hands tightened on the wheel. "I'm not sure."

"You never did say much about the blind date. Other than you didn't want to talk about it."

Jeremy shoved the back of the passenger seat with his knees. "Take the hint, Haley."

"It's okay, Jeremy." Andy drew a deep breath. "Haley, it wasn't a good idea to play that kind of trick on us. Adult relationships are complicated, and that didn't help."

Haley crossed her arms, clearly not buying it. "I think you're both being stubborn."

"Haley!" The passenger seat rocked again.

"I'm serious. They're perfect for each other, but they won't do anything about it." She shook her head, and her braids whipped around her shoulders. "It's ridiculous."

"I'm sorry, Pastor." Jeremy's deep voice resonated through the sudden silence in the car. "I've told her to try thinking *before* talking sometimes."

"Haley, it's like this." Andy flipped on his blinker as he took the highway exit. "You know I care for Lori. But I'm not so sure she feels the same way about me."

"Baloney."

Andy checked over his shoulder before changing lanes. "I'm serious."

"I heard her ex showed up this weekend."

Andy met Jeremy's gaze in the rearview mirror as the teen spooned another bite of apple cobbler into his mouth. "How'd you hear that?"

"Small church. Word travels."

He was right—and usually, it traveled even faster than that German chocolate cake had disappeared at the potluck. Andy braked at a red light and rubbed his temples with his fingers. He couldn't believe he was sitting in a car discussing his love life—rather lack of—with two of his youth-group members. Friends or not, mature or not, it was pathetic. Andy's head throbbed, and he rubbed harder.

"I didn't mean to upset you," Haley said. "I'm sorry. I have a really big mouth."

"It's okay, Haley," Andy answered wearily. "I just need you to lay off the matchmaking. I'm getting enough of that from the deacons' wives and the church widows."

A slight thud sounded in the backseat. "Whoops, dropped my bowl."

"Napkins are in the cubbyhole. You better not leave sticky cobbler on my floor mats," Andy warned.

"No problem, Pastor. I've got it." Jeremy's head disappeared behind the seat as he leaned over to clean the mess.

"Speaking of deacons, isn't that Mr. Sinclair?" Haley tapped the passenger window with her finger, then waved.

The older man in the car next to them stared.

Andy leaned over in a wave, but still no response.

"He must not recognize us." Haley waved harder.

The light turned green. Andy tried another wave without acknowledgment as he accelerated through the intersection. "Oh, well. How's that cobbler coming, Jeremy?" He darted another glance in his rearview.

Jeremy's head popped up. "I think it's okay, but it's too dark to tell for sure. I'll get some carpet cleaner at Haley's house."

"I'd appreciate it."

"Turn here." Haley gestured at the next block. "Second house on the right."

Andy made the turn and pulled into Haley's long driveway. The teens climbed out and hurried inside to find the cleaner, leaving Andy alone to wait as the scent of apples wafted through the car.

Too bad Lori had never showed. She could have taken Haley home, and he could have driven Jeremy, and this horrible, embarrassing talk about his relationship status would have never happened. No, scratch that. If Haley and Lori had ended up alone to talk… Andy shuddered. That would have been worse. He supposed all things happened for a reason, after all.

He rested his head against the back of the seat and sighed. Every now and then, he just wished something *good* would happen for him, too.

The glass doors of the bank closed behind Lori with a whoosh of wind, effectively shutting out her dreams. That was the third bank she'd visited during her extended lunch hour Monday, and they all presented the same horrible equation. Not enough credit plus no cosigner equaled no loan, no way—even if she was a "nice girl" with "good intentions." The proposal she drew up hadn't helped a bit.

A harsh winter breeze blew through her hair, and Lori shoved the dark strands behind her ears as she headed for her car. Looked as if she had no backup plan once Bella returned, after all. In a few days, she'd be right back where she'd started from.

Lori yanked open the door and collapsed behind the steering wheel, unable to muster the energy or motivation to crank the engine. It didn't help her mood any that she hadn't talked to Andy since that disastrous phone call Saturday before her dinner with Jason.

No, she definitely wasn't doing so hot in the man department. She'd chickened out of going to church yesterday, afraid of her feelings and afraid of what seeing Andy might do to her bruised heart. So she'd stayed in bed with her Bible and notepad, reading through the book of Psalms and trying to keep her mind off the men in her life and how the only one she really wanted to care about her suddenly didn't seem to mind that her ex had reappeared in her life. She shouldn't wish jealousy on someone, especially not a friend, but the fact that Andy was *just* her friend was the whole problem in the first place. What made her not good enough to be more than a friend? Why hadn't he even considered it before? She'd hoped Jason's reappearance in her life would finally open Andy's eyes.

But by the way he'd stood by and let Jason railroad her at Café Du Monde, it wasn't likely.

Lori rested her forehead against the wheel and tried to calm the anxious beating of her heart. No love life. No loan. No dreams.

No paycheck.

She groaned. Maybe since she'd spent so many years at the Aquarium of the Americas, they could fit her in somewhere. Her old job managing the gift shop had been filled, but at this point, cleaning floors and fish tanks would be better than staying unemployed and furthering her credit-card debt. At least she'd be able to work with Gracie again.

Lori turned the key in the ignition and waited while her car puttered to life. Was that all she had to look forward to? Making a barely tolerable salary doing a job she hated while hoping to catch glimpses of her friend in an upper-management state?

She sat back in the seat and cranked on the heater. Whom was she kidding? Everything would be different now that Gracie and Carter were married. It was just a matter of time until she'd have no job, no money and no best friend. She closed her eyes. Add no boyfriend or future husband to that growing list.

Her cell phone jangled from the cup holder, and she considered not answering. But even a telemarketer's company beat wallowing in this deep-sucking bog of self-pity. She shook off the claws of depression before they could sink in further and flipped open her cell. "Hello?"

"Lori, it's Jason."

Just when she thought her day couldn't get any worse. She turned the heater down to better hear him through the sketchy reception. "What do you want?"

"That glad to hear from me, huh?"

"Get to the point, Jason." Lori sniffed, then pressed her fingers against her lips. She would *not* cry on the phone with her ex.

Jason cleared his throat. "Listen, I just wanted to apologize for offending you Saturday night. That was never my intention. And, also, I'm calling to tell you I have a proposition."

Lori's eyes popped open. What kind of—

"A business offer." Jason's voice softened. "I really think you'll want to hear it."

At this point, she was desperate enough to do just that. At least if it was business, it wasn't personal. Lori's fingers clenched around her phone. "All right, I'll hear you out. But no guarantees."

"No problem. Where should I meet you?"

"Why not just tell me now?"

Jason hesitated. "I think it'd be better in person."

"Fine." Lori jerked the gear into reverse and began backing out of the parking space, narrowly missing an SUV. "I'll be back at the Chocolate Gator in just a little bit. Meet me there."

Jason's relieved sigh sounded through the line. "Great, I know you won't regret—"

"You'll have ten minutes." She closed her phone and tossed it on the passenger seat as she merged into traffic.

She wouldn't let him have the upper hand with her again.

Andy knocked on the door of the head pastor's office, heart pounding an erratic rhythm that matched the anxious tapping of his hand. He hadn't been summoned to Pastor

Mike's office since that time two years ago when the youth group nearly destroyed the gymnasium after a rained-out football game gone bad.

He shifted his weight and knocked a second time. Maybe it wasn't bad news. Maybe the budget committee had formulated raises for the staff, or maybe Pastor Mike just wanted to check on the status of the Spring Retreat. But if that was the case, why wouldn't he pop into Andy's office the way he usually did? Even when Pastor Mike spoke with him about the staff wanting Andy married off, he came to Andy and tried to make the visit casual.

Andy swallowed hard. No, this couldn't be good at all.

"Come in." The senior pastor finally answered Andy's knock, and his solemn tone didn't bode well for Andy's nerves. He slowly stepped into the room. The late-afternoon sunbeams streaming through the slanted blinds provided the room with a false sense of gaiety.

"Close the door behind you." Pastor Mike swiveled in his black leather office chair, a grave expression on his face. "Please have a seat."

Both requests sounded more like demands, and Andy's pulse raced as he quickly obeyed. He knotted his fingers together in his lap and waited, not sure what to say or what might make things worse. The ticking of the engraved clock on the desk sounded like a time bomb waiting to explode.

"We have a situation on our hands." Pastor Mike leaned forward, bracing his arms across the cherrywood desk. "One I hoped to never have to address in this church."

Andy's nerves tingled. Apparently when he messed up, he messed *up*. The question was, what had he done? He shuffled his feet against the plush carpet, afraid to speak lest his voice sound like he'd just sucked in a balloon full of helium.

"Frankly, I'm more than a little surprised." Pastor Mike steepled his fingers and stared at Andy with an unblinking gaze. "I thought you knew better than this, especially considering the recent hoopla in the news."

Andy blinked twice, unable to get past the fact that his pastor had actually just said the word *hoopla*, and even more confused as to what he was talking about. "Sir, I'm sorry. I don't understand."

"You know it's against church policy to ride alone in a car with a female member of the youth group."

Andy frowned. "I haven't, sir. I abide by that policy and all the others."

Pastor Mike's bushy eyebrows rose. "That's not what a source tells me."

"What do they say?"

"That last night after church, you gave Haley Jergens a ride home, unattended." Saying the words out loud seemed to foster the pastor's anger even more, and his voice deepened. "You know that is inexcusable. I personally would never assume anything untoward came from such a mistake, but considering the recent events of—"

"Pastor, if I may." Andy held up one hand. "I wasn't alone with Haley. Her longtime boyfriend, Jeremy, was also with us in the car. His truck broke down in the parking lot, and I gave them both a ride. I took Haley home first."

A wrinkle formed between Pastor Mike's eyes. "A trusted source tells me otherwise."

Andy's mind raced, trying to think who from the church could have seen them in a car alone. Then it hit him. "Deacon Sinclair. Was he your source?"

Pastor Mike hesitated.

"He was at a red light next to us. We waved, but he never waved back. I thought at first he didn't recognize us, but now I guess he was upset."

"But if he saw you, why would he not see Jeremy?"

"The cobbler!" Realization dawned, and Andy stifled a

laugh at the absurdity of the situation. "Jeremy dropped his dessert in the backseat of my car. I bet he was bent down cleaning it up right at the time Mr. Sinclair looked over." Andy held up both hands in surrender. "I promise it's the truth, sir. You can even check my floor mats for cobbler stains. I doubt Jeremy got it entirely clean."

Pastor Mike's cheeks reddened. "No need. I believe you. I'll correct the misunderstanding right away with Deacon—uh, with my sources."

"Thanks." Andy offered a slight smile, though his insides still trembled at the close call. "Is that all?"

"Yes. I do apologize for this mishap."

"I understand." Andy stood and made his way to the door. "It was an honest mistake."

"You're doing a great job here." Pastor Mike's quiet voice made Andy pause. "I hope all of this hasn't discouraged you too much."

Andy forced his head to shake. "Not at all."

"But you haven't forgotten about our talk regarding marriage?" Pastor Mike held his breath.

"I haven't forgotten." How could he, with the constant reminders? "It's just not as easy as one might think." Andy clenched his teeth from saying more. Talk about an understatement. That was sort of like saying Hurricane Katrina was a mild thunderstorm.

"Oh, of course not." Pastor Mike shuffled papers on his desk, an obvious attempt at looking preoccupied. "I do have to point out, however, that if you weren't single, these rumors wouldn't have been so quickly believed."

Andy's stomach tightened, and he nodded again. "Have a good afternoon, Pastor."

"You do the same."

Andy slipped into the hall, pulling the door shut behind him with a solid click. He leaned against the thick wooden door and released a heavy sigh. First the entire church staff wanted him married; now they were starting rumors about his misconduct with his youth group?

Tears of stress pressed behind his eyes, and Andy pinched his nose with his fingers. Maybe he should quit. He obviously wasn't going to win Lori anytime soon, not with Jason back in town and claiming credit for Andy's romantic attempts. If he couldn't have Lori, he didn't want anyone. And if that were the case, the staff would only let him stay on for so much longer before kicking him out. They might not actually ever fire him for being single, but at this rate, they'd make his life so miserable—intentionally or not—he'd quit of his own accord. How could he work for and share a ministry with staff members who didn't trust him? If the only way to gain their trust was to marry, then they apparently were all in for a long wait.

Andy slowly trudged down the hall, his shoes squeaking against the shiny linoleum. He'd go back to his office and pray about turning in his resignation before this entire ordeal grew worse and he ruined his reputation—or worse yet, the reputation of one of his teenage charges. He couldn't work so guarded like this, so on the edge all the time. He needed to give his full attention to the teenagers and to his job, not constantly be looking over his shoulder wondering who would be next to misinterpret his every action.

## Chapter Twenty

Lori set two napkins, two cups of coffee and a plate of cherry bonbons on the table in front of Jason. A gooey chocolate barrier between her and her ex—nothing safer than that. She plucked a candy from the plate as she sank onto a chair opposite him.

"I'm glad you agreed to talk with me." Jason folded his hands on the table, ignoring the chocolate and coffee and giving her his full attention.

She nibbled on the candy with a frown. Why couldn't he have shown such devotion years ago when they dated? Now he was looking at her in the same way she imagined him once having looked at Amy. Lori hated to keep reliving the past, but every time she saw Jason, she saw his betrayal. It was one thing to forgive and forget from miles away, knowing she'd never see him again. It was quite another to sit across from him and not scream every mean thing she'd ever written in her diary.

She chewed harder, trying to relax. The cherry crème melted on her tongue, and Lori released a slow breath. She really shouldn't freak out on Jason again until at least hearing what he had to say. After all, her current options were somewhat limited, and who knew? Maybe he could save the day after all. He'd shown through the thoughtful gifts that he could be a decent person. The least Lori could do was swallow her pride and hurt feelings for the next few minutes and hear him out. "What'd you want to discuss?"

A smooth grin slid across Jason's face. "Other than the fact that I love when you wear your hair up?"

The chocolate suddenly tasted dry in Lori's mouth, and she fought the urge to pat the messy bun she'd created after leaving the bank. She swallowed hard. "Yes, other than that." Business, she had to keep this just business. Otherwise Jason would suck her in again before she had a chance to think twice—which would be precisely his goal. "You said you had a *business* proposition."

"You're right." Jason fingered the edge of his ceramic coffee mug. "But the two are sort of related."

"How so?" Lori picked up another bonbon, nerves clenching her stomach. She tried to keep her expression neutral as she chewed.

"You want to start your own business, right?"

"Right."

"And you're not financially capable at this time, right?"

"Thanks for the brutal reminder, but, yes. I actually just left a bunch of laughing bankers in my wake." Lori narrowed her eyes, remembering the smirk on the loan officer's face as he reviewed her credit scores.

Jason leaned back in his chair, pausing to take a sip of coffee. "I have a way we can both get what we want."

Lori's hopes jumped despite the fact she knew there had to be a catch. "How so?"

"I've spoken with my father, and we've agreed that a business run by Lori Perkins would be worth investing in. We can front you the money. Think long-term loan, with zero interest. How does that sound?" Jason's eyes twinkled over the edge of his mug.

"I think it sounds too good to be true." Lori crossed her arms over her chest. No way was it that simple. Jason never offered something for nothing—not his time, his energy or his heart. She'd learned that the hard way when he wanted something she refused to give before their wedding—so he found it with someone else.

"There is a catch." He ducked his head.

"I figured."

"If you agree to this business loan, we'd get you all set up. Prime real estate, supplies, materials, employees, the works. You'd pay us back a certain percentage as you drew in a profit, from the bottom line." Jason drew a deep breath and set his mug on the table. "And in return, you forgive me."

"You think it's that simple?" Lori shook her head. "What, are you in a twelve-step program or something? Am I check-mark on your list?" She scooted her chair back and stood.

"Lori, I'm giving you an opportunity to live your dream. All I'm asking is that you quit hating me, see that I've changed." Jason leaned forward, his eyes pleading. "I'm trying to move on. I really am a good guy. I wish you'd give me a chance to prove it."

"You've proven plenty over the years."

Lori began clearing the plates from the table, her heart racing at Jason's proposal. There had to be an ulterior motive. He couldn't care about her forgiveness that much. How could he even know she'd held on to that grudge this long? No, there was something else at stake, a card he wasn't ready to play. She could almost see it peeking from underneath his sleeve.

Lori banged two plates together as she turned for the counter. She was done with his cheating games. "I think you'd better leave." No business opportunity was worth getting mixed up with Jason again.

Jason slowly stood and slung his leather briefcase strap over his shoulder. "Just think about it, okay? It'd be great—for both of us." He paused until she looked at him, then offered a gentle smile and walked out of the shop.

Lori sank back into her chair at the vacant table and buried her face in her hands. She couldn't believe Jason and his father had the nerve to make such an offer. She couldn't believe she'd sat right there and listened and not slapped him across the face.

But mostly, she couldn't believe that tiny piece of her heart that was actually considering the idea.

Andy shut the door to his office and headed down the hall toward the sanctuary, Bible in hand. He should go pray and get his head together before the service started. He had an hour before the kids showed up. Even if Andy left without any answers, just being quiet for a while would hopefully deplete the stress that had consumed him ever since his talk with Pastor Mike.

Andy took the long way toward the sanctuary, past the secretary's office and through the outdoor courtyard. He took a long breath of chilly night air, letting the cold sink into his skin through his thin long-sleeved shirt. It was a little colder than usual for mid-February. Last year on Valentine's Day he remembered wearing short sleeves and sandals. This Valentine's was just a few days away, not that his bruised heart needed the reminder. The weather wouldn't really matter, though, seeing how he'd spend the day at church and then holed up alone in his apartment, trying to rid his mind of the image of Lori out with Jason.

Andy yanked open the double doors to the sanctuary, stress already knotting his shoulders. *God, I really need to focus. Please help me.* He couldn't keep torturing himself this way. Lori hadn't even talked to him since their phone call last Saturday at the movie theater. It was clear she wanted time to spend with Jason.

The heat seeping through the church warmed Andy, trimming the sharp edge off his thoughts. He soaked in a small measure of peace as he quietly made his way down the dim aisle, past rows of vacant pews toward the altar. He'd sort all this out in prayer and hopefully be able to focus on his pending sermon.

A bowed head in the third row caught Andy's eye, and he slowed his pace, not wanting to interrupt what appeared to be fervent prayer. He sneaked a peek at the loyal parishioner as he passed, then gasped at the familiar locks of chocolate-brown hair. "Lori?"

She looked up, red-rimmed eyes brimming with unshed tears. "Hey, stranger."

The cozy-warm church suddenly felt burning hot, and Andy tugged at the collar of his button-down shirt. There was so much he wanted to say, wanted to ask. Hope sparked inside that maybe this was his answer from God at last. But it was all he could do to choke out a greeting. "Hi."

Lori wiped her eyes with her sleeve and sniffed. "How are you?"

Silly question coming from a woman crying. Andy's counseling instincts took over, and he slid into the pew next to her, forgetting the awkwardness of the moment. "I'm fine, but you're obviously not. What's up?"

"Nothing. Just…thinking."

"Lori." Andy inched closer and brushed her hair away from her tearstained cheek. "Talk to me. I know things have been a little weird between us lately, but I'm still the same old Andy."

Lori hesitated. She turned her head to look toward the altar, the church's dim lamps highlighting the natural streaks in her hair and turning them amber. Andy held his breath and waited. Would she confide in him at last and bring their friendship back to what it was? Or was this it—their final goodbye?

Andy gripped the back of the pew in front of them with his free hand, the other still lightly resting on Lori's shoulder. He had no intention of moving it until she gave him a sign. He craved contact with her, anything to show him she still cared, even if it was only as a friend.

When Lori spoke, her voice was quiet, her gaze never leaving the front of the church. "It's Jason. He's made me an offer."

Andy's stomach twisted painfully. "What kind of offer?" *Please don't say marriage, please don't say marriage.*

"A business deal. He and his father want to invest his father's money into my own shop." Lori smiled but it didn't reach her eyes. "It's everything I've always wanted."

"So, are you going to do it?" Andy's hand dropped from her shoulder and fell limply to his lap. He couldn't believe Lori would consider getting mixed up with her ex again financially, even if she was desperate to manage her own store. Would she really sacrifice her values for the sake of some business deal? He wasn't stupid. Jason would hold that financial tie over her head until he got something from the arrangement, too. His stomach churned imagining what.

"I don't know." Lori finally turned and met Andy's gaze. "He wants me to forgive him, but I think there's more to it than just that."

A fist socked Andy's stomach. Of course there was more to it. Jason wanted her back. No man hopped the border to another state to offer his ex-fiancée money without a reason. "Oh?" He forced his voice to stay neutral.

"I can't trust him emotionally. How can I financially?" Lori let out her breath in a long sigh. "But I have to be logical. I'm about to be out of a job when your aunt comes home, and I need a new plan. Maybe this is God's provision."

Lori's voice held equal levels of doubt and hope. Andy drummed his fingers on the back of the pew, hating that Lori teetered on the cross beams of wise and foolish, and he wasn't able to do a thing about it. But he just couldn't sit back and let her make this mistake. Forget waiting for clarity, forget waiting on Lori to decide what or who she wanted. It was time to make a move. Time to finally share his heart.

"Before you agree to anything rash with Jason, there's something I have to say." Andy tucked a strand of hair behind Lori's ear, cupping her cheek with his hand and gently turning her face toward him.

She inhaled sharply at his touch, and his hand shook as he stared into her eyes. "I—I know this is really sudden, but please. Don't say yes to Jason."

Lori's eyes darted back and forth, studying his with an intensity that made Andy forget to breathe. He pressed on before he lost his nerve. "Say yes to me."

"What—what are you asking?"

Andy had a planned response, but it escaped him as he stared at her mouth. Instead, he asked the only question that filled his mind. "If I can kiss you."

Lori's lips parted, but before she could do more than nod, Andy leaned in and pressed his mouth to hers.

## Chapter Twenty-One

Lori's eyes widened, then slowly closed as the realization of Andy's kiss sank in. She kissed him back, a mixture of shock, relief and joy melting together like chocolate into one fantastic dessert. His hand buried in her hair, and she tilted her face to his, never wanting the moment to end.

The subtle yet pointed sound of a throat being cleared echoed through the sanctuary, and Lori jerked away, breathless. Pastor Mike stood in the center aisle behind them, a grin teasing his features. "Pardon me. But this might not be the proper time or place for such a personal display of affection."

"Sorry, Pastor." Andy stood and drew Lori up with him. Her heart hammered and her knees shook, from both the kiss and the embarrassment at being caught. She awkwardly reached up and patted her hair, hoping it wasn't mussed.

"No need to be embarrassed." Pastor Mike rocked back on his heels, one hand jingling the loose change in his pocket. "I just was coming in to practice my Wednesday-night sermon." He kept grinning.

They were grown adults, caught kissing in the middle of the church, and all Pastor Mike could do was smile? Where was the lecture? Lori frowned.

Andy led Lori up the carpeted aisle toward the back doors. "We'll get out of your way, Pastor." He squeezed Lori's hand, and a flock of butterflies suddenly took up residence in her stomach. "I need to go over my sermon as well."

The pastor winked at Andy and clapped his shoulder as they passed. "I knew I shouldn't have worried about you, boy. Good choice!"

The doors to the church shut behind them. Lori paused in the foyer and tugged on Andy's hand. "What did he mean by that? What choice?"

Andy threaded their fingers back together and pulled her hand up to his chest. "Nothing important." He ran one finger down her cheek and smiled. "Nothing like this."

A blush heated her cheeks. "So what does *this* mean?"

"I don't know. I'm still waiting on your answer to my question."

"If you could kiss me?" Lori laughed. "I think you got your answer."

Andy's eyebrows meshed. "Oops. I mean, the question I never got to ask." He smiled. "What do you think about us dating?"

Lori reached up and clasped their joined hands with her free one. "I'm thinking that sounds like a much better offer than Jason's business proposal."

"Are you sure?" Andy edged back a step so he could look her in the eye. "I can't give you money and your own store and make all your dreams come true like—"

Lori pressed one finger over Andy's lips. He immediately hushed. "I don't need all those things to be happy if I'm with you."

"Really?" Andy's mouth brushed against her finger. "You've felt the same way about me all this time? I only realized it myself a few weeks ago."

Lori nodded. "I always figured you never thought of me as more than a friend, so I didn't say anything. Then that Friday at movie night, when you almost kissed me…" Her voice trailed off, and her cheeks burned at the memory. "I felt so foolish."

Andy groaned and rested his forehead against hers. "I wanted to kiss you so badly that night, but I thought it was too soon. I thought you were mad at me for even trying. Plus there was that thing you said a year or so ago about not dating after Jason."

Lori shook her head. "I think we've had quite the communication problem."

Andy wrapped his arms around her in a gentle hug. "Not anymore."

Lori closed her eyes, enjoying the warmth of his embrace. After all this time, she was finally where she belonged. She snuggled closer and breathed a sigh of satisfaction. Who cared about her secret admirer now that she had Andy? That mystery man was too late, and she didn't mind a bit. *Thank You, Lord.* She never would have thought when she came to the church to pray about Jason's proposition that she'd end up in Andy's arms.

"While we're being honest, there's something else I need to tell you." Andy's breath whispered against her hair, and a shiver skated down Lori's spine. "You know those gifts—"

The lobby door opened, and Pastor Mike stepped through the opening. "Sorry to interrupt again. I left the last page of my sermon on my desk." He headed toward the front doors, then winked at them over his shoulder. "I guess everything works out for a reason, huh, Andy?" He smiled and didn't wait for an answer before disappearing outside.

A new kind of shiver raised the hair on the back of Lori's neck. "What is he talking about? What's going on?" She edged away from Andy with a frown.

Andy shook his shaggy hair out of his eyes. "It's a long story I never got to tell you. It's funny, really. Pastor Mike came to me a few weeks ago, saying that because of the pressure from some of the teens' parents and the scandal at that church across town, the staff was concerned that I was single and wanted me to change that." He laughed. "Crazy, huh? They gave me the impression my job depended on it, but it wouldn't have gone that far. I don't think so, anyway."

Lori slowly pulled her hand free of Andy's grasp and backed up a step, bumping into the foyer display table and rattling a vase of fake flowers. "A few weeks ago?"

"Yeah, right about the time you started working for Aunt Bella." Andy paused. "What's wrong with that?"

Nothing, other than it was conveniently about the same time Andy said he'd realized his feelings for her. Lori shook her head and withdrew farther, wrapping her arms around herself. The warmth flowing from the church's heating vents did nothing to ease the sudden chill creeping over her body. "You don't want me. You just want to keep your job."

"What?" Andy stepped forward, but Lori scooted farther away. He gave a short laugh. "Lori, no. That's not it."

She rubbed her arms. "Yes, it is." A wave of insecurity washed over, freezing her to the core. "I was the only potential prospect you had, so you went for it. Isn't that right?"

Andy frowned. "Yes, you were the only one I was interested in, so of course I didn't go for anyone else. But—"

"So it's true."

"Yes. No! I mean…" Andy rubbed his hands down the length of his face. "What are you asking?"

"Forget it." Lori dug her keys from her pocket and pushed through the lobby doors to the parking lot. Andy followed, calling her name, but she picked up her pace and quickly slid into her car. She pushed the button for the automatic locks just as Andy yanked on the handle.

He pounded on her window. "Lori, don't leave like this!" His muffled voice pleaded through the window, but all Lori could hear was Jason confessing his relationship with Amy. Then Monny's voice piped in her memory, announcing he had a fiancée and, no, he wasn't interested in her. They were never interested. She was destined to forever be the friend, the *almost*—never *the One*. Andy just proved that cold fact again. How dare he judge her for considering Jason's business offer when his was no better? He just wanted to show the staff he'd finally found a girl so they'd back off. More than likely, it wasn't even a coincidence Pastor Mike had showed up when he did. Andy probably planned the whole thing. He'd been that desperate to keep his job—at her expense.

Lori yanked the car into reverse and peeled out, tires squealing against the gravel. Tears slipped from her eyes and rolled down her face. With blurry vision, she glanced in her rearview. Andy stood alone in the parking lot, hands on his waist as he stared after her. She cranked up the volume on the radio to drown the voices of rejection in her head.

Andy's was the loudest of them all.

Andy somehow made it through his sermon, even though his mind was dozens of miles away with Lori. Perhaps even farther than that—at the rate she'd peeled out of the parking lot, she could be halfway to Georgia by now.

While the youth band led the service's closing song, Andy made his way offstage and to the kitchen in the back of the gym. Gracie stood behind the counter, opening packages of cookies and setting out plates and napkins for the kids. At least he had one volunteer tonight. Lori's sudden absence could have really left him in a chaotic position if not for Gracie.

The red-haired newlywed took one look at Andy's face and dropped a bag of chips. "What happened?"

"That obvious, huh?" Andy turned his back to the stage and propped his elbows on the counter, briefly burying his face in his hands. The pounding of the drummer's beat reverberated through the gym and vibrated his arms.

"You talked to Lori." It was a statement, not a question.

Andy lifted his head. "She already called you?"

"No, but I figured it had to be about her to make you look

that depressed. Did she not respond as you hoped?" Gracie ripped open the bag of chips and poured them into a plastic bowl.

Andy snagged one and popped it in his mouth. "Actually, she responded better than I could have hoped—until Pastor Mike showed up, made a few comments that started Lori asking questions and ruined the entire thing." Andy quickly explained what had transpired in the sanctuary only hours before, including the business offer Jason had made. "Now Lori thinks I only was interested in her for the sake of pleasing the staff and keeping my job."

"That's crazy. You would never do that." Gracie's eyes narrowed. "Would you?"

"Of course not. You know me, Gracie. Come on." He reached for another chip.

Gracie sighed. "You're right. I'm sorry. This whole secret-admirer game just threw me off. I still think you should have been honest with her sooner. How did Lori take that news?"

Andy stopped mid-chew. "Um…"

Gracie planted both hands on her hips. "Are you kidding me? You haven't told her yet?"

"I tried." Andy swallowed. "Pastor Mike interrupted us, and then she stormed off before I could explain."

"So why are you still here? Go after her!"

"Uh, the youth service?" Andy raised his eyebrows.

Gracie's lips twitched. "Oh, yeah. Well, as soon as it's over, go find her. Lori needs to know the truth about those gifts. If she knows they're not from Jason, she won't be nearly so trusting of him. You've got to tell her the truth before she does something crazy—like accept his proposal and sign paperwork."

"Do you really think she would? Even after our kiss?" Surely it had meant something to Lori. It certainly meant something to him—the epitome of every dream he'd ever hoped for and then some. If she didn't feel the same… Andy's stomach cramped.

"Well, I didn't witness this earth-shaking kiss of yours,"

Gracie replied dryly, "but I know Lori, and I know her insecurities. If she's hurt down to a certain level, there's no telling what she might rationalize."

Andy glanced over his shoulder just as the closing note of the worship song rang through the speakers. The teenagers began spilling out of the rows of chairs, hurrying toward the food. "Here comes the herd."

"Listen, I can handle this." Gracie stacked some plastic cups beside the two-liter drinks. "Go find Lori."

"Are you sure?" Doubt and hope meshed as one as the kids swarmed around Andy at the counter. He wanted to stop Lori and explain everything before it was too late, but his first duty was here at the church. Then again, Gracie could chaperone things until the parents came to pick up their children....

"I'm positive. I'll call Carter if I need to." Gracie waved her hands as if flicking him away. "Go save the day, Pastor."

"I owe you one." Andy grabbed his keys and headed for the door before the noisy mob of teens could change Gracie's mind.

He had a girlfriend to catch.

## Chapter Twenty-Two

The alarm sounded way too early for Lori's preference. She pushed her hair out of her eyes and slapped the snooze button before burrowing back under the covers. Her head throbbed, her eyes felt grimy from crying herself to sleep and her neck was sore from all the tossing and turning during the night.

That's what she got for ignoring Andy's knocking on her door. He pounded for fifteen solid minutes yesterday evening before giving up. She'd spent the time sitting on the floor in the living room under the front window, back pressed against the wall, torn between wanting him to leave and hoping he never would.

With a groan, Lori sat up in bed, shoving the covers off her legs. She couldn't go back to sleep with thoughts of Andy tormenting her. Her anger from yesterday still boiled beneath the surface, along with a variety of other feelings she couldn't quite name. Betrayal, frustration, confusion. None of which seemed to completely sum up her emotions or do her feelings justice.

A glance at the digital clock confirmed that she'd better jump in the shower, or else she'd be late for work. Lori rubbed her hands over her cheeks, deciding not to peek in the mirror on the way to the bathroom. If she looked anything like she felt, the mirror would probably break.

She stood, stretching, and something crumbled under her feet. Bending down, Lori grabbed the balled-up piece of paper from the floor and slowly peeled it open. It was the pro/con list for accepting Jason's business offer that she'd hastily scribbled last night.

| PROS | CONS |
|------|------|
| Open my own store | Be tied to Jason financially |
| Live my dream | Lose independence |
| Have a secure job | Lose Andy's friendship for good |

That last entry had been made during the brunt of her anger. Mascara streaks dotted the wrinkles in the page from the abundance of tears she'd cried, and Lori quickly threw the paper in the trash before stepping in the shower.

The steam from the hot water did wonders for clearing her mind. Lori poured a puddle of shampoo in her hand and rubbed it through her hair. If the potential of Andy was gone forever, there was really no reason why she shouldn't call Jason. He had a point—everyone won. She'd have her own business and could begin working on climbing out of debt. So what if Jason had a catch to the deal? Even if he wanted her back, it wasn't like she *had* to date him. She could muster up the energy to forgive Jason if he was truly willing to invest in her dream.

And who cared if Andy got mad in the process?

Lori adjusted the water temperature and turned so the spray could massage the tension knots in her shoulders. Jason's business proposal wasn't any worse than the secret motive behind Andy's offer. At least Jason had been up front with his intentions. Andy hid his away and pretended to have feelings for her.

Though that kiss had certainly said otherwise.

The memory burned hotter than the water blasting on her neck, and Lori quickly shut off the faucets. So what if Andy could kiss? She'd been kissed before, and this time wasn't any more life-changing than any other time.

But it certainly could have been had Andy not ruined everything.

She slipped into her pink terry-cloth robe and cinched the ties at her waist. She'd call Jason right now and ask him to meet her at the shop today to tell him she accepted his proposal.

After yesterday's disaster with Andy, the sooner the better.

There was a line of hungry people waiting at the shop when Lori arrived. She shouldered past the crowd to unlock the door, muttering apologies for being late, and flicked on the lights.

"I'll be right with you!" She hurried behind the counter, tossing her purse on the shelf and flipping on the coffee machine so it could brew. "Monny, you back there?"

*"Si."* He poked his head through the swinging doors and smiled. "Already started today's pastries."

"You're a lifesaver." Lori tied her new pink apron around her waist, keyed in her access code on the cash register and smiled at the gentleman standing patiently in line. "How may I help you?"

The next two hours slid by as a steady stream of customers flooded the shop for morning coffee, chocolate croissants and fudge. Lori placed ten special orders for Valentine's Day, all before noon. She breathed a heavy sigh and leaned against the counter. "If it's already this busy today, I dread tomorrow and Saturday."

"It will be—what do you call it?—a madhouse. Valentine's Day is special." Monny snagged a bottle of water from the fridge by the storage closet. "What are your plans?"

A month ago, Lori would have thought his question was an invitation. Now she knew better. "Probably not much. I'll go to church and maybe afterward visit my parents. I bet you miss your fiancée this time of year, especially."

Monny nodded, sadness tainting his smile. "I do. But we'll

be together in a few months." He toasted his water bottle at her and disappeared back inside the kitchen.

Business finally at a lull, Lori took the time to wipe down the counters with a wet rag. Summer would be in this afternoon to help manage the cash register and clean, but the mundane action gave Lori time to think.

Jason hadn't answered her call earlier this morning, so she'd left a voice mail. Now she was waiting, something she once promised herself she'd never do for him again. She'd waited enough in the past for calls that never came, for dates that were hours late because he'd been with Amy. She'd waited for him to show up at church and family dinners—usually to no avail. Even if it was just business, why was she still waiting on him?

Lori scrubbed at a stubborn spot on the counter with her damp cloth. Maybe starting and managing her own store wasn't worth the risk of finding out Jason hadn't changed after all and had an ulterior motive. She was taking a huge leap of faith, and for what—dreams? Money? When had she become that desperate?

She closed her eyes. Probably about the same time her credit cards had neared their limits and the loan officers had laughed at her proposal—which was actually still in her purse. She couldn't bear throwing it away, not after having spent so many hours preparing it.

Lori tossed the rag in the sink with more force than necessary. People started businesses every day. Why was her proposal such a risk compared to theirs? Determination clenched her teeth. She would do whatever it took to prove those bankers wrong.

The chime on the door tinkled, and Lori looked up—just in time to see Jason, Andy and Aunt Bella stroll inside.

Lori's face paled lighter than the white chocolate samples displayed on the counter. Andy watched as her eyes darted from one face to another, lingering on Jason longer than anyone else.

He tried to ignore that proverbial slap as he made room for

Jason to pass him. Andy couldn't help butting shoulders with him as the loser moved toward Lori with a welcoming smile.

Andy tugged on Aunt Bella's arm. "We might need to give them a minute." He'd picked Bella up from the airport an hour earlier at her surprise phone call announcing her return. Of course she wanted to pop in to the store before going home. Who knew Andy's timing would be so perfect they'd literally bump into Lori's ex on the way in?

Bella's wise eyes took one look at Andy and then at Lori, now talking in hushed tones with Jason over the counter, and she snorted. "Nonsense." She cleared her throat. "Lori, hon. I'm back!"

Lori smiled weakly. "Hi, Bella."

"Things look wonderful. How's business? We haven't talked in a week or more." Bella bustled around the far side of the counter and joined Lori by the register. "Sales are good?"

Lori stepped aside to make room as Bella flitted around. "We've been booming the last several days."

"The week before Valentine's is always that way." Bella stopped and tugged at the front of Lori's apron. "This is cute! Your idea?"

Lori's shoulders straightened a little. "Actually, yes."

"Love it. What else have you done?"

Andy smiled as Lori's confidence bloomed before his eyes. She eagerly pulled out a notebook and began showing Bella what sounded like sales records. His happiness faded, however, at the sight of Jason waiting by a vacant table, hands in his pockets, whistling as he rocked back and forth on designer leather shoes. That easygoing stance showed way too much confidence—borderline arrogance, in fact.

Maybe Lori had told him that Andy spent fifteen pathetic minutes knocking on her door last night. On his way here with Bella, Andy had managed to convince himself it was because she'd been in the shower or already asleep for the night. But now, seeing that smirk on Jason's face… Andy's fists clenched, and he took a deep breath before his temper made him do something he'd regret.

"Do you have some sort of a problem?" Jason's rocking stopped as he squared off with Andy, apparently having finally noticed his staring.

Andy stepped closer, determined not let this guy think he was intimidated. His heart thundered in his chest. "Actually, I do, but this isn't the time or place." He refused to get into an argument with Lori in earshot.

"I'm sorry you feel that way." Jason smiled, flashing a row of perfect white teeth. "I, on the other hand, feel great."

Andy faltered at the unexpected response. "What—why?"

"Lori accepted my offer to fund her new business. In a matter of weeks, she'll be running her own shoe store in the French Quarter—and if I have anything to say about it, accompanying me around town at the same time. This is such a fun city, isn't it?" His grin spread. "I can't wait to see it with her." He began to whistle once more, turning toward the back of the shop to watch Lori.

Andy wanted to punch that cocky smirk off Jason's face, but his arms suddenly felt like noodles. Lori had made her decision.

He was too late.

Lori watched Bella study her proposal. The shop owner had been so excited about the changes Lori had created in her store that she wanted to hear it all. With a burst of courage, Lori had pulled the proposal from her bag and presented it to Bella.

Now Lori stood, chewing on her lower lip and wishing she could snag a chocolate crocodile from the case as she watched Andy and Jason square off. They were pretending they weren't, but the truth was obvious. Her heart hurt, wondering what Jason might be rubbing in Andy's face. Even if Andy had hurt her and used her, there was no cause for cruelty—and that gloat on Jason's face represented exactly that.

Was Jason telling Andy she'd accepted his business offer? When the three of them had walked inside the store, her shock momentarily wavered her confidence in her decision—that, and seeing Andy's face again. His kiss still hovered in her memory like her favorite fleece blanket, soft and warm. But she'd asked Jason to meet her, and she couldn't let a fleeting feeling change her resolve. She was making the right decision. Jason had shown so much effort to prove he'd changed, with the gifts and all, that he deserved her forgiveness.

And she deserved her dream.

Bella slid her reading glasses on top of her head and turned piercing blue eyes to Lori. Her lips pursed, then broke into a giant smile. "This is brilliant."

"It is?" Lori's mouth opened. "I mean, thank you." Excitement temporarily replaced the tap-dancing nerves. "You're the only one to think so."

"What do you mean?" Bella's penciled eyebrows drew together in a tight frown.

Lori explained her bad luck with getting a loan. "I'm too much of a risk."

"That's ridiculous. I should go down to those banks and tell them what-for."

"I appreciate the loyalty, but it's hopeless." Lori hesitated. "With my current credit, I guess it's my fault."

"I'll have to see what I can do about that." Bella tapped the proposal in her hand. "Now, how about my nephew over there?" She nudged Lori in the ribs. "I saw hearts in his eyes a few minutes ago. Now I understand why he got all flustered every time he called me about the store."

"You know about that?" Lori winced.

Bella laughed. "Andy confessed he told you. I hope you weren't upset with me for asking him to keep an eye on the store. Of course I trusted you with it, or else I wouldn't have hired you. But it was the only way I knew to get you two together."

"What?" Lori's mouth gaped open. Bella had been scheming as a matchmaker, too? Was the entire city of New Orleans trying to get her and Andy together? She snapped her mouth shut.

Bella's eyes twinkled. "He would always talk to me about Lori this, Lori that. I knew he had a thing for you months ago, even if he didn't see it himself yet. It seemed like destiny when you turned up needing a job just when I needed a store manager."

Lori's own heart skipped before thudding painfully against her chest. "Andy had a thing for me months ago?" Months. Not just weeks. Not just since the pastor's ultimatum. Her eyes darted to Andy and Jason, who now stood yards apart as if they'd never even met.

"That was my interpretation." Bella handed the proposal back over and met Lori's gaze. "And I can assure you, my dear, that I'm rarely wrong."

# Chapter Twenty-Three

Lori fiddled with the strings on her apron as Bella breezed out of the shop, unable to do more than call a faint goodbye in her wake. Andy held the door for his aunt and then turned, sending a sad smile in Lori's direction. The depth of emotion in his eyes made Lori open her mouth, eager to stop him and apologize for her outburst at the church Wednesday night. Then Jason cleared his throat, and the reminder of her decision hit full force. She couldn't go into business with Jason now if she and Andy had a chance together.

Lori looked back at Andy, but he was gone. The door shut behind them with a snap, and a thick silence fell over the shop.

Jason joined Lori on her side of the counter, slipping off his coat and tossing it on the shelf. "Alone at last."

"Actually, Monny is still in the kitchen." Lori tapped the pages of her proposal together although they were already pretty straight. Hopefully Monny wouldn't leave for lunch before Summer arrived for her shift. Lori didn't feel comfortable being alone with Jason, especially not with that eager gleam in his eye. Should she get rid of him, cancel the whole deal? But what if Andy refused to give her a second chance? Part of Lori wanted to run after Andy and beg forgiveness for overreacting. The other part of her—the logical, realistic, soon-to-be unemployed part—feared his rejection and whispered doubts laden with insecurity.

Lori forced a smile through the turmoil. "What's the first step?" She wanted to draw up papers or go real-estate shopping. Something. Anything to convince herself she was making the right move.

A slow smile quirked Jason's lips. "I think the first step should be a hug—and maybe a kiss." He held out his arms and moved toward her with an enticing smile. "What do you say? For old time's sake?"

Lori ducked away from his reach, and Jason's arms fell to his sides. A frustrated frown marred his features. "Come on, Lori. We're a team again. What's the big deal?"

She jerked as if he'd slapped her. "It's a very big deal. You haven't earned my trust back. This is a business to me, Jason. Business *only*. I'm not interested in being partners with bene-fits, regardless of our past."

His expression hardened, then softened as if he'd flipped a switch. "I'm sorry. You're right." He straightened and edged away, respecting her space. "Let's take a look at that proposal you have and see what kind of goals you're after."

Lori pressed her lips together and took a deep breath before handing over the proposal.

Jason flipped open the first page. "This looks great. Very professional."

"Thanks." Her shoulders straightened. "I did it myself."

"You did a good job."

This was new—compliments on her efficiency from the very man who once ruined most of the confidence she'd ever had. Lori's defenses melted a little further. This was the smart choice. It had to be. She smiled. "I just might have to celebrate my new business with some shoe shopping tonight. I can use my gift card."

Jason nodded absently as he kept flipping pages.

"The gift card you got me."

"What?" He looked up, eyebrows scrunched together in confusion.

Lori reached for her purse to show him. "You know, the one you sent when you were my secret admirer."

"Oh, right. That one." He smiled, distracted, as he looked back at the proposal. "Hope you enjoy it."

Lori tucked the gift card back in her purse. Something didn't feel right. Was Jason that preoccupied with her proposal? He almost sounded like he'd never seen the present in the first place.

Time for a test. Lori tugged the proposal from his hand. "That was really romantic, you know, playing the role of secret admirer. It was what helped convince me to forgive you and give you a chance with this business deal."

"Glad to hear it." Jason reached for the papers, but Lori held them back, forcing him to keep eye contact.

"What was your favorite of the presents you sent?"

His cheeks colored. "The gift card, of course. I remembered how much you love shopping."

"Second favorite."

Jason sighed, clearly growing frustrated. "Why does it matter?"

"Just curious." Lori kept the proposal out of reach and waited.

"The, uh…the teddy bear." He sniffed and snatched at the document in her hand. "Now can we get back to work?"

Lori let the papers slide through her fingers as anger fused with shock. She'd never received a teddy bear. A fact that could only mean one thing—Jason wasn't her secret admirer.

Her eyes narrowed at Jason's profile as rage and a fresh burst of regret reeled her senses. He'd lied to her, again. He hadn't changed—if anything, he'd gotten worse. She didn't want anything to do with this man. Not with his money, or his time. How could she have ever considered going into business with him? Her stomach rocked at the close call, and she grabbed her proposal. "Get out."

"What? Lori, are you insane?" Jason stared in surprise. "What's wrong with you?"

"You are." She shoved his jacket at him. "My secret admirer never sent a teddy bear. You lied to me."

"I said what I had to say to get you to talk to me." Jason stumbled over his feet as Lori kept pushing him toward the door. "I know this is the right decision, if you would just—"

"I said go—before I call the police."

"The police?" Jason gawked. "Lori, what's gotten into you? You've never been this rude before."

"Guess I learned from the best. Thanks for teaching me." She pushed open the front door and held it with a pointed expression. "Goodbye, Jason."

"You can't give up on her." Bella's tone offered little room for arguments from the passenger seat of Andy's car.

His fingers gripped the wheel harder as he made the turn onto his aunt's street. "You don't understand. She made her decision."

She *tsked* with her tongue, flapping one hand in the air as if brushing off a fly. "Women change their minds all the time. It's our prerogative."

Andy bit his lip to keep back the frustration threatening to pour forth as he pulled into Bella's driveway. "You know you're my favorite aunt, but will you please give it a rest?" He couldn't take much more of the prodding. Bella hadn't stopped since the moment they'd left the shop. It was like ripping a bandage off his heart with every word.

Bella opened the door as the car rolled to a halt. "I will certainly not give it a rest. My favorite nephew is in love, and I'm going to make sure his heart doesn't get broken." She shut the door behind her and walked to the trunk.

"I'm your only nephew," Andy muttered as he unlatched his seat belt. He joined Bella at the trunk of his car and picked up the largest of her suitcases, her words echoing through his head. *I'm going to make sure his heart doesn't get broken.*

Andy hefted the suitcase into the house, duffel bags hanging off each arm. Too late for that.

Summer's eyes grew rounder and rounder. "I'm a measly half hour late for work and I miss all the good stuff." She shook her head, blond hair brushing fast across her cheeks. "I can't believe Jason lied like that."

"I can." Lori locked the door of the Chocolate Gator and slipped her keys into her purse. "He always did before." She pressed her fingers against her eyes, wishing she could erase the entire day. Looking back, the whole afternoon seemed surreal. First Bella's unexpected return, Jason and Andy butting heads, and then discovering Jason's lies. She wanted to go home and hide under the covers, but maybe an evening stroll would clear her mind. "Do you want to take a walk with me? I need some air."

"Sure." Summer fell into step beside Lori, and they walked the first block in silence, enjoying the quiet, cool night air.

Lori tugged her jacket tighter around her, trying not to look in store windows as they ambled through the French Quarter. Red and pink hearts decorated almost every display, a harsh reminder that Valentine's Day was right around the corner. She'd been single the last few years at the dreaded V-day, but she always had Gracie and Andy to order a pizza with or rent a sappy movie to make fun of together. Now Gracie had Carter, and Andy—well, Lori had lost that friendship along with everything else she thought she was sure of this afternoon.

"Why are men so clueless?" Summer offered the question into the evening air.

Lori shrugged. "Some things we'll never know." She let out her breath in a slow huff. "Sort of like how I'll probably never know who my secret admirer was."

Summer's eyebrows knitted together. "I guess that is still a mystery, huh? I grew so used to the idea of it being Jason, I forgot we still have no idea."

"I wish I could forget."

"Come on, you don't regret the gifts, do you?" Summer paused in front of the window of a music store and admired the display promoting iPods. "Oh, look, the new version is out."

Lori pulled on Summer's jacket sleeve to tug her along. "No, I don't regret getting the gifts, not really. But if I hadn't gotten them, I would have never agreed to this deal with Jason. I really thought he had changed."

"Forget about that. Nothing you can do now." Summer shoved her hands in her coat pockets. "Maybe your secret admirer is a stranger, some random customer that saw you working that first day in the shop and thought you were cute."

"Maybe." Lori shivered as a sudden gust of wind lifted her hair from her coat collar. But she didn't want a stranger, she wanted Andy. "Wait, that's impossible. The gifts were so personalized, he had to have already known me."

"Then I'll tell you what I've told you a hundred times already. It's Andy."

Lori shook her head. "No way."

"Why not?" Summer stopped walking and faced Lori, crossing her arms stubbornly across her chest. "You've been so determined this whole time that it couldn't be him. I don't understand why you're so adamant about it."

*Because nothing that great ever happened to her.*

The truth rocked Lori's senses, and she stopped beside Summer, a new chill washing over her that had nothing to do with the winter breeze teasing her hair. After Jason broke off their wedding, she'd started looking for the negative in everything. Why waste precious time and energy on something she wanted so badly just to get shot down again?

Summer started walking again. "Quit assuming you know everything and give the idea a chance."

Lori didn't want to go there in her mind, not after the emotional drama of the afternoon, but Summer's silence made it impossible not to. Andy knew she loved chocolate— Wait a minute. The Hershey's Kisses. She stopped walking again, and her mouth gaped. Andy always kept a bowl of them on his desk in his office at the church. The corny cards—pure Andy. The new leather Bible cover—he'd seen her ripped and faded one at church a hundred times. Of course he'd know her favorite verse. And the gift card for the shoes—well, anyone could have known that.

But the sweet note that came with the last gift… Lori closed her eyes, the words still memorized, lingering in her brain. *To the woman who makes more lists than anyone I've ever known—just one of your many adorable qualities. Here's a supply to get you through the next few pro/con situations.*

The truth hit Lori's heart like Cupid's bow, and a slow smile teased the edges of her lips until it blossomed into a full-fledged, goofy grin.

Andy really was her secret admirer.

## Chapter Twenty-Four

Lori tried to squelch her excitement as she poured two cups of coffee and took them to the table where Bella waited. The shop owner had called her that morning and asked to meet before the store opened to discuss business. Maybe Bella was going to let Lori stay on a little longer. At least until she could put out her résumé and find a decent paycheck—especially since Lori's dream of running her own store was no longer possible, thanks to a horde of snobby bankers and her lying ex-fiancé.

She pushed away the negativity that still hovered with thoughts of Jason. Eventually, she'd have to forgive him. If she didn't, that grudge would only fester and spoil her own life—not his. It was obvious Jason had no true regrets about anything. It was better to brush him out of her life once and all—even if the forgiveness factor still left a bad taste in her mouth.

It sure would be a lot easier to forgive him if she had something positive to cling to—like a relationship with Andy. Why hadn't he answered her calls last night? Lori tried to focus as she sat in the chair opposite Bella. Now wasn't the time for wishing. It was time to get to business. She drew a deep breath. "Need any cream or sugar?"

"Black is fine." Bella took a long sip. "Mmm, perfect."

"It took a while to get there." Lori wrinkled her nose. "Your coffeemaker didn't like me at first."

"Lucille is ornery," Bella agreed.

"You named the coffee machine?"

"A monstrosity like that deserves recognition. Don't you think?"

"Maybe that's why she never liked me. I didn't know her name." Lori grinned around her mug.

"Well, regardless of Lucille's stubbornness, you rose above and conquered your obstacles. I'm very impressed." Bella leaned back in her chair and studied Lori with a serious gaze. "I left you in a tough spot. No training, little instruction. Yet you did an amazing job."

Lori blinked and set her mug on the table. "I did?"

"Certainly. Sales increased from last quarter, and I can't walk down the street without one of our regulars telling me how much fun they had visiting with you. They also mention how much Summer has changed, how friendly and lighthearted she is now." Bella shook her head with amazement. "You're like a supermanager."

It couldn't be that easy. Doubt tickled the edges of Lori's newfound confidence, and she nervously traced the rim of her coffee cup with one finger. Maybe she had made a difference in befriending Summer, but the sales record had to be a mistake. She hated to remind Bella of her many managing errors, but Lori had to know. "What about all my mess-ups? Forgetting to close the freezer and losing a day's worth of customers, burning ingredients, a flopped three-for-two sale…" Lori's voice trailed off as Bella waved her hand in the air.

"Everyone makes mistakes. Two months after I opened the store, I nearly burned the place down when I forgot to turn off the oven. Life happens, Lori. It's what we make of it that counts—and you have made this business something worthwhile over the past several weeks." Bella smiled. "So I'd like to offer you a full-time management position, under a few conditions."

Lori's heart soared so high she thought it might never come back down. She had a job! It wasn't managing her own store, but that could come in the future after she raised her credit scores and padded her savings accounts. This way she could draw a decent paycheck, pay off her debt and get to keep hanging out with Summer and Monny.

Her hopes danced a little higher. Who knew, if she stayed at the shop, maybe she'd eventually convince Andy to give her another chance. Between church and the Chocolate Gator, he'd have to talk to her eventually. Whatever conditions Bella had up her sleeve would be well worth the benefits. Lori leaned forward in her chair. "What conditions? I'll do anything!"

"I thought you might." Bella's eyes twinkled. "The first condition is that you must implement all the ideas you had in your proposal. Your plan for selling logo merchandise in the store is pure genius. Make it happen."

"Really?" Lori's mouth opened in surprise. "The tote bags, coffee mugs, aprons, flip-flops—"

"The works." Bella nodded. "Just use the company credit card to get started, and I have a hunch profits will pay off in a few short months. The second condition is you have to agree to consider buying the shop from me when I retire. You'll have about three years to prepare."

Lori reeled backward. "You're retiring?"

"Spending time with my family in north Louisiana made me realize how much I miss them. I'd like to move there eventually, and this agreement seems ideal. It gives me a few years to get some affairs in order, and gives you time to save your pennies for buying me out." Bella winked.

Lori's mind whirled as the reality of what was happening settled around her. She was not only going to keep managing the Chocolate Gator, she was going to get to own it in a few short years! This was even better than starting her own business from scratch—she'd have instant clientele and little risk of failing. God had answered her heart's desire, and in an even better way than she could have hoped for. Lori blinked hard against the sudden onset of happy tears. "Is that all?"

"Yes, on the business end. But I do have a personal request."

"Anything."

Bella scooted her mug out of the way and reached for Lori's hands across the table. "My Andy is quite smitten with you. I know there have been some misunderstandings, but the boy is miserable."

"I know." Lori lowered her eyes. "I've tried calling him, but he's avoiding me." She licked her lips. "I don't know what else to do but wait."

"Don't give up." Bella squeezed her hands, then released them with a smile. "You're a smart girl. You'll figure something out."

Saturday afternoon, Andy pulled his car into the church lot and parked in his usual spot. The gym would be deserted today, and he could play a little basketball in peace and try to forget the events of the last two days. Lori had tried to call his cell three times since Thursday night, but he couldn't bring himself to answer. Once she and Jason started a business partnership, it was probably only a matter of time before they fell in love again. He couldn't stand hearing her talk about how happy she was with Jason and their new arrangement. He also couldn't stand Bella's pushing, so he'd ignored her calls the past two days as well. Andy loved his aunt, but one more "Don't give up on Lori" and he might rip his hair out by the roots.

Andy fiddled with the lock on the gym door until it finally opened, then helped himself to the storage closet full of sports equipment. The steady thumping of the basketball against the hardwood floor felt comfortably familiar, and he swished an easy three-pointer. Now, why couldn't he play like that when the kids were watching?

He nailed another shot, and then practiced a few layups. Ten minutes later, a fine sweat coated his forehead, and the ball felt slick against his palms.

"Dude, I'm open!"

The deep voice startled Andy away from his game, and the ball bricked against the rim. Jeremy stood at one side of the court, hands out. Andy tossed him the ball. "What are you doing here?"

"It's Saturday. Haley's at some cheerleading thing, so I thought I'd see who was hanging out here. I tried your cell to get you to meet me, but you didn't answer."

Andy dug his phone from his pocket. He'd silenced it after Lori's last call and forgot to turn it back on. He turned the volume up. "Sorry about that."

"Why was it on mute? I thought you only did that during church services." Jeremy nailed a perfect layup, then rebounded the ball to Andy.

Andy dribbled twice and shot. It hit the backboard and bounced left. "You want honesty, or the easy answer?"

"Honesty." Jeremy caught the basketball and threw it back.

Andy missed again. "I'm avoiding Lori."

"I thought you were chasing Lori."

"Plans changed. She has a new…business partner." The words left a stale taste in Andy's mouth. He didn't want to think about how Lori and Jason would spend Valentine's Day—cozied up somewhere romantic, to be sure. Jason the Jerk probably wouldn't even notice Lori would wear her red polka-dot heels like she did every Valentine's Day. He didn't deserve her. Andy threw the ball with extra force, and it sank through the net with hardly a swish.

"You should play angry more often." Jeremy tossed a three-pointer. "So, what are you going to do to win her back?"

"Win her back?" Andy stopped in the middle of the court and bent over, panting. "What do you mean?"

Jeremy hooked the ball under his arm and paused in front of Andy. "Whenever Haley's mad at me, I always do something nice to win her over. You know, something romantic like flowers or candy." He rolled his eyes. "Girls like that stuff."

Andy stifled a laugh at the words of knowledge coming

from this high-school jock. But funny or not, Jeremy had a solid point. Girls did like that stuff, especially Lori. Would Jason keep up the romantic charade Andy had started with the secret-admirer game? Or would he eventually reveal his true colors?

It didn't matter. Lori had made her choice. "It's too late for flowers, man."

"It's never too late," Jeremy argued. He spun the ball on his finger and watched it wobble. "One time Haley thought I was into this other girl, but it was a stupid misunderstanding. A large order of fries and a dozen roses later, I was back in the game."

It would take more than a few French fries to convince Lori he had pursued her because of love and not for the sake of his job. But maybe something a little more creative could work. Would she even listen to an attempt?

Andy had to find out. One more try before he accepted reality and admitted defeat. It was almost Valentine's Day—a guy could hope, couldn't he? Andy clapped Jeremy on his shoulder as he jogged past him toward the back door. "I think I know just the thing. Thanks!"

He needed a sheet of paper and a pen.

Lori flicked on the lights inside the Chocolate Gator, checking her watch for the third time since leaving her house. She had just enough time to bag up a variety of chocolates for Andy before church started. She needed to get there a little early, as she'd have her hands full today, helping out in the youth department, fielding broken hearts from teen girls still unnoticed by their crush and convincing the guys it was okay to share their mushy feelings with their girlfriends one day out of the year.

Hopefully before the chaos began she'd have a chance to find Andy and give him a personalized valentine—a bag of mixed chocolates, and her heart. Plus a little something she'd prepared on her new stationery.

Lori worried her bottom lip between her teeth as she slid open the display case. Since Andy had avoided her calls all weekend, this little V-day delivery of hers could go either way. But she had to try. Whether he took her back or not, Andy had to know that Jason was no longer in the equation and she knew the truth about the gifts. It was his decision how he chose to respond.

She'd better quit thinking about it or she'd chicken out.

Lori grabbed one of the new pink-and-black bags she'd special-ordered for Valentine's Day and shoveled a mix of Andy's favorites into the sack. Caramel creams, chocolate-drizzled marshmallow puffs and, of course, a few chocolate crocodiles. She topped the order off with a cherry crème bonbon, tucked the special note inside and stapled the bag shut.

A timid knock sounded on the front door. Lori swiveled toward the entryway and nearly dropped the bag of goodies. Andy peered through the glass, shading his eyes with one hand. She hid the bag behind her back and threw the dead bolt to open the door. "Andy! What are you doing here?"

He stepped inside, shoving aside a shock of sandy hair that had fallen in his eyes. "I got your note asking to meet me here."

"I didn't send a note." Her heart trembled at his nearness, and she edged away a step so she could breathe. No one but Andy had ever had this effect on her senses. She drew a shaky breath.

"Yes, you did." Andy whipped a handwritten card out of the pocket of his khakis. "It says right here to meet you at the shop before church."

Lori bit back a smile. "That's Haley's handwriting."

"Haley? How did she—" Andy briefly closed his eyes. "Jeremy. I played basketball with him yesterday."

Lori couldn't help but laugh. She should have known better than to tell Haley her plans for surprising Andy. The meddling little matchmaker had begged for an update yesterday. With Lori still soaring high from the good news about her job, she'd confessed more than she probably should have.

Though this particular act of matchmaking might have been for the best. Now Lori could give Andy his gift in private and not risk the embarrassment of being watched at the church. Her grip tightened on the bag, and the paper rustled.

"What's that?" A shadow fell across Andy's face. "Something for Jason?"

"No." Lori swallowed and held the sack out to Andy. "It's actually for you. I was going to surprise you at church, but thanks to Cupid's little helpers, this might be a better time."

"For me?" Andy's eyebrows arched. "What about—"

"Jason isn't in the picture anymore." Lori took a step closer. "I tried to call you and tell you all weekend, but you never answered."

The Adam's apple bobbed in Andy's throat. "I thought you were calling to talk about your new relationship."

"Relationship?" Lori snorted. "I never would have considered dating Jason again. I was in it for the business angle only." She sighed. "Although I don't think he ever got that particular memo."

Andy frowned. "I thought since you were going into business with him that you two would—"

"It never crossed my mind." Lori held up two fingers.

Andy gently tugged them down. "You were never a Scout."

"It's still the truth." She smiled, then lowered her gaze. "Listen, Andy. I know you're my secret admirer."

"You figured it out, huh?"

She tilted her head to one side. "Why did you let me believe it was Jason all that time?"

Andy reached up to rub the back of his neck with one hand. "I thought you were glad it was him. Then, when he made you that business offer…" Andy shrugged as his voice trailed off. "It was too late. I was too late."

"No, you're not." The whisper rushed through Lori's lips, and Andy's eyebrows raised.

A wave of nerves washed over Lori like a tidal wave, and she suddenly felt shy. "Sit down. Open your gift—it will explain everything." She moved to a table nearby and sank onto the seat, hoping Andy wouldn't notice her shaking hands. She pasted on a smile and waited while he tore into the paper sack.

"Chocolates." He popped the bonbon in his mouth and gave her a close-lipped grin. "My favorite."

Lori relaxed. There was her best friend, the Andy she knew—talking with his mouth full. "There's something else." She inhaled. This was it. The moment of truth where they'd either pick up where they left off in the church sanctuary and make this day the best Valentine's ever…or go to church with broken hearts and a ruined friendship. It was all up to Andy.

"No, wait." Andy stood and dug into his pocket. "I have something for you, too. I wanted to give it to you last night, but then I got your note—well, Haley's note—asking to meet you this morning and decided to wait. Since its Valentine's Day and all…" His voice trailed off, and he handed Lori a slip of notebook paper. "Sorry it's not fancy."

Lori slowly unfolded the lined paper. "What is this?"

Andy knelt beside her chair and pointed to the two columns. "A list of pros and cons to being in a relationship with me."

Lori scanned the list, pressing one hand against her face to hide the slow smile spreading across her cheeks as she read.

| Pros | Cons |
| --- | --- |
| I'll treat you like a queen | I can be immature |
| You'll never run of chocolate | I talk with my mouth full |
| I already know all your secrets | Sometimes I snore |
| I'll always let you have the remote | I'm cranky after a nap |
| You're my best friend | I'm a horrible basketball player |

Andy cleared his throat. "The lists came out even, so I understand if you're not interested."

"Actually, I made a list for myself about being in a relationship with you." Lori dug the stationery out of the bag of chocolates on the table and handed it to Andy. "See for yourself."

He took the chocolate-smeared slip of paper, his slight frown morphing into a wide grin as he read. "There's only one entry, and it's on the pros side."

Lori wrapped her fingers around Andy's, covering the note with her hand. "It's you. That's the only reason I need."

Andy stood quickly, pulling Lori up beside him, and gathered her in his arms. "You know I would never use you, don't you?"

Lori nodded as tears pricked her eyes. "I've always known that. I'm sorry I doubted you."

"And I'm sorry it took me so long to see what was right in front of me." He tucked a strand of her hair behind her ear and leaned in so his breath whispered across her cheeks. "I love you, Lori. Job or no job, business or no business, I love you. I always have."

"I love you, too." Lori welcomed his kiss, tightening her arms around his neck. He pulled away, and she smiled. "You taste like chocolate."

"Add that to the pros side of the list." Andy grinned before covering her mouth with his own again. "Happy Valentine's Day, Lori."

She let out a happy sigh before snuggling deeper into his embrace. "Happy Valentine's Day."

And this year, it truly was.

# *Epilogue*

"Hey, no kissing on my couch." Carter threw a gummy bear at Lori and Andy from his position in the chair across the room.

Lori ducked away from the onslaught and laughed. "You guys started it." She pointed at Gracie's bulging stomach. "About six months ago, I might add."

Gracie tossed back her red hair and grinned. "I always knew you'd make a great aunt." She patted her stomach as she reclined back against the love seat. "Only three more months."

Carter tossed the remote control to Andy, who nestled beside Lori on the couch. "Here. I have a feeling movie night is about to become a chick flick if someone doesn't man up. These women will be chatting about babies and weddings all evening if we don't stop them."

Andy aimed the remote at the television and pressed several buttons. "I don't think this controller has that kind of power."

Lori held up her left hand and admired her ring finger. The diamond glistened in the glow of the lamplight. "What's wrong with talk about weddings and babies?"

"Yeah, it's not like you guys are innocent in all of this." Gracie shoved a pillow behind her back. "Whew, that's better."

"You think you have it rough now, Carter? Wait until Carter

Junior or Little Gracie appears and you're walking the halls at midnight." Lori threw the gummy bear back at Carter.

He caught it and grinned. "Hey, as long as Junior is willing to play the guitar one day, I don't mind a little crying."

Gracie rolled her eyes. "He keeps saying that."

"Like you don't wish your little one will grow up to work in the aquarium?" Andy quirked his eyebrow at Gracie.

She reddened. "At least I don't say it every ten minutes."

"Shh, the movie is starting." Carter pointed to the TV. "No more baby talk for the next two hours." He cut a glance at Andy and Lori from the corner of his eye. "Or smooching."

Gracie clicked off the lamp, and everyone settled in for the movie. Andy nuzzled Lori's hair, and she leaned back against him with a soft sigh. "I can't believe all that's happened in a year."

"I know." Andy's breath warmed her cheek. "Last Valentine's Day we were just starting to date. Now we're engaged. Maybe next year we'll be expecting our own baby. Who knows what God has planned for us?"

Lori snuggled closer as the opening credits of the movie rolled. "I don't care what we do, as long as we're together."

Andy pressed his lips gently against the top of her head. "Happy Valentine's Day. I hope I get to tell you that for the next fifty years."

"You'd better." Lori smiled at the diamond on her finger and then angled her head toward his. "I want a real kiss."

"Are you sure you want to risk Carter's wrath?" Andy rubbed his nose against Lori's.

"I'm not scared." Lori wiggled her eyebrows up and down.

Their lips brushed sweetly together. Then they simultaneously ducked the next round of gummy bears.

\* \* \* \* \*

Dear Reader,

I hope you had as much fun reading this book as I had writing it. I knew as soon as Lori made her first appearance in *Return to Love* that she needed to share her own story. She and Andy seemed to be the perfect match from the very beginning, and I had a blast putting them together.

Valentine's Day has always been one of my favorite holidays. Some argue that it's simply a commercial holiday, a manipulated attempt at getting consumers to spend money on things they don't need in order to express their feelings. But I say celebrating love and romance is fun! What's better than red-and-pink window displays, heart-shaped candy, mushy greeting cards and, of course, a ton of chocolate? Some of my fondest memories from my school-age days were sending Snoopy or Care Bear valentines to classmates and indulging in pink-frosted cupcakes.

It's good to show our spouses and friends that we care about them, but in the midst of celebrating earthly love, we need to always remember the gift that was demonstrated through the death and resurrection of Jesus Christ—the *true* lover of our souls.

Blessings!

Betsy St. Amant

# QUESTIONS FOR DISCUSSION

1. The book begins with Lori feeling overwhelmed and in desperate need of chocolate. What is your favorite comfort food?

2. Lori and Andy were best friends for years before realizing their feelings for each other. Have you ever had a close relationship with a person of the opposite sex and suddenly discovered you had feelings for them?

3. Andy thought sending gifts as a secret admirer would warm Lori up to the idea of his being boyfriend material instead of simply friend material. Was this a good idea, or did it just cause more problems later in the story?

4. Have you ever had what you thought to be a good idea backfire and create issues in your life?

5. What was your favorite of the gifts Andy sent Lori as a secret admirer? Why? If you were to send surprise gifts to someone, what would you send?

6. When Jason showed up and lied about the gifts being from him, why didn't Andy object?

7. How did Andy's staying silent create more problems for him and Lori?

8. Lori was tempted to accept an offer she knew wasn't right for her because it would propel her toward a longtime dream. Have you ever had to choose between right and wrong at the risk of sacrificing a specific dream or goal?

9. Andy worked at the church as a single youth minister. Do you agree or disagree with the staff for pressuring him toward marriage?

10. Lori's befriending her coworker Summer helped turn the younger girl back toward God. Have you ever reached out to someone who was a little different than you to share the gospel? If so, what happened?

11. At first, Summer's hardened appearance of dark clothes, tattoos and piercings turned Lori away. How are appearances often deceiving? What efforts can we make to ensure that we never falsely judge someone?

12. Lori had a special love for shoes. Do you have a favorite accessory or item of clothing that you always look for when shopping?

13. Two of the teenagers in the youth group played a part in putting Lori and Andy together. Did their matchmaking schemes make things easier or harder on them? Should the teens have gotten involved, or stayed out of it? Why or why not?

14. Lori dreaded the approach of Valentine's Day because she was going to be without a date. Have you ever been in that position during a holiday? What did you do to celebrate alone?

15. Lori's knack for design helped land her the permanent management position at the Chocolate Gator. If you were a customer at the shop, what sort of logo merchandise would you suggest Lori sell?

*Read on for a sneak preview of*
*KATIE'S REDEMPTION*
*by Patricia Davids,*
*the first book in the heartwarming new*
BRIDES OF AMISH COUNTRY *series*
*available in March 2010*
*from Steeple Hill Love Inspired.*

*When a pregnant formerly Amish woman returns*
*to her brother's house, seeking forgiveness*
*and a place to give birth to her child,*
*what she finds there isn't what she expected.*

*P*lease, God, don't let them send me away.

To give her child a home, Katie Lantz would endure the angry tirade she expected from her brother. Through it all Malachi wouldn't be able to hide the gloating in his voice.

An unexpected tightening across her stomach made Katie suck in a quick breath. She'd been up since dawn, riding for hours on the jolting bus.

Her stomach tightened again. The pain deepened. Something wasn't right. This was more than fatigue. It was labor.

Breathing hard, she peered through the blowing snow. It wasn't much farther to her brother's farm. Closing her eyes, she gathered her strength.

*One foot in front of the other. The only way to finish a journey is to start it.*

She sagged with relief when her hand closed over the railing. She was home.

*Home.* The word echoed inside her mind, bringing with it

unhappy memories that pushed aside her relief. Raising her fist, she knocked at the front door. Then she bowed her head and closed her eyes, grasping the collar of her coat to keep the chill at bay.

When the door finally opened, she looked up to meet her brother's gaze.

Katie sucked in a breath and then took a half step back. A tall, broad-shouldered Amish man stood in front of her with a kerosene lamp in his hand and a faintly puzzled expression on his handsome face.

It wasn't Malachi.

*To read more of Katie's story,*
*pick up KATIE'S REDEMPTION*
*by Patricia Davids,*
*available March 2010.*

*Love Inspired*

After two years away, Katie Lantz returns to her Amish community nine months pregnant—and unmarried. Afraid she'll be shunned, she's shocked to meet carpenter Elam Sutter, who now owns her family farm. Elam and his kindly mother show Katie just what family, faith and acceptance truly mean.

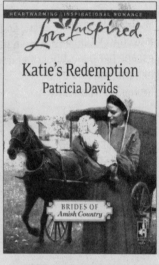

HEARTWARMING INSPIRATIONAL ROMANCE

*Love Inspired*

**Katie's Redemption**
Patricia Davids

BRIDES OF
*Amish Country*

Look for
# Katie's Redemption
by
# Patricia Davids

*Available March wherever books are sold.*

**www.SteepleHill.com**

Steeple
Hill®
LI87583

# LARGER-PRINT BOOKS!

**GET 2 FREE
LARGER-PRINT NOVELS
PLUS 2 FREE
MYSTERY GIFTS**

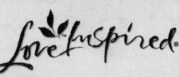

## Larger-print novels are now available...

LILP10